MW00576068

Distant Cousin

by

Delia Drake

North
Country
Press

Distant Cousin

ISBN 978-0-945980-87-2

Library of Congress Control Number: 2015931219

North Country Press
Unity, Maine

This book is dedicated to Austin Brann Sr., my husband, who encouraged me to fly, and in memory of Adrian who sat with me for hours.

Chapter 1

Aunt Sue died today. She was a nice woman. I used to love to go to her big old house and play in the upstairs tower room with a cupola that sat right on top of the three story house overlooking Rigby Cove on a wide peninsula. We always referred to it as the kupp-a-la. My Aunt Wanda and Uncle Hal would bring the family to visit a couple times a year and sometimes I was allowed to stay with her a few weeks in the summer to give Aunt Wanda a break from me.

My name is Thea. I don't know what my last name is because I was found on Aunt Wanda's doorstep when I was two days old. I had been raised as a distant cousin under the name of Thea Chadworth. Aunt Wanda probably would have taken me to the nearest orphanage, but I came with a written guarantee. Attached to my blanket was the name of a lawyer with a phone number. The only information he would give Aunt Wanda was that she would receive a check every month until I was through with my education. I would have sufficient funds for all my needs. The check that Aunt Wanda got for taking care of me was enough for them to move to a large house in Trafton, Maine, and it made it easier for her and Uncle Hal to raise their own family—their daughter Carry who was four at the time and their son Tony who was six. The Chadworths didn't exactly love me, but I was tolerated in a grateful way. The only really great times were spent at Aunt Sue's. She was Uncle Hal's sister and was sort of a recluse. She wasn't weird or anything, she just liked her privacy. She was a writer and spent a lot of time in her office. Nobody ever knew what she wrote or what name she used. I never found any books by Susan Chadworth, so I guessed she used an alias.

Aunt Wanda had called this morning all atwitter to tell me the news. She said Aunt Sue had fallen off the widow's walk and also that there would be no funeral. She was full of the fact that the

Chadworths would inherit Aunt Sue's estate. They figured that Carry and Tony would have a tidy little nest egg.

I was very sad to hear the news. I now sat on my front steps and considered how I could convince the police that Aunt Sue had been murdered.

Chapter 2

The phone rang again and I went into the house to answer it. I loved my little house. I had purchased it two years ago when I had gotten a bonus from my job as head librarian. I had come back to Trafton after college as it was the only roots I had and immediately was hired at the new library. I had graduated with distinction from a small liberal arts college and was delighted to get the position. I worked very hard to put our library on the map so to speak. The board was pleased and told me often. I had shared my news with Aunt Sue in a letter and she had written back that she knew I would do a good job. She had given me a recommendation after all. The Chadworths didn't care one way or the other. Their interest in me had waned when the checks stopped coming after I left for college. The lawyer had stipulated that I had to have high academic achievement to get the college money and I strived to make it so. I was smothered under the feeling of being an obligation as a distant cousin in both senses of the word and needed to accomplish something in my own right. Of course, everyone including me was very curious about who I was and how I would end up. As soon as I was employed gainfully the money stopped. Carry and Tony had labored through high school and swore they would never again pass the door of a school. They both were still at home and worked out—Tony at the Chadworths' local hardware store and Carry filled in when they needed help.

The phone call was from Carry. She was enthusing about the family going over to Rigby for the reading of the will. She said the lawyer had mentioned that I should attend as she imagined there would be a small remembrance for me. I said I would drive over on my own—I wanted to try out my little, used VW. The little car handled like a dream and I was so glad I had listened to my friend Emmy and bought it. I arrived ahead of my cousins and sat in the car to wait for them. When they pulled up in the Cadillac that my aunt had just bought, they affected an attitude of affluence that they really didn't have. I was kind of embarrassed but thought, oh well they soon will have. They greeted me with indifference and I followed them in to the first level of the building that housed Henry Severied, Aunt Sue's attorney. I had met Mr. Severied before at Aunt Sue's and he greeted me with a warm smile and handshake as he did the others. He said that several people were still to come and we sat, quietly on my part and fidgety on the Chadworths'. Before long Mrs. Ames, Aunt Sue's cleaning lady and Perry, her gardener arrived and Mr. Severied put on his glasses and began. I sneaked a sad smile at Mary Ames and Perry Dawson and they smiled back at me; we were old friends from way back. I always loved to spend time with them as Aunt Sue was usually closeted in her study, and they more or less took care of me both inside and outside the big house. Carry and Tony elected not to visit Aunt Sue without their parents and were standoffish with the hired help. To me it was paradise. I felt like I was wanted for myself and not just the money paid for my keep. I hadn't seen Mary and Perry since I started at the library and they looked a little older to me.

Mr. Severied cleared his throat and began to read. Mary and Perry were left money outright and the right to remain at their jobs if they so chose. The Chadworths exchanged sour looks and I feared for Mary and Perry's positions. Mr. Severied looked over his glasses at the Chadworths and they smirked back at him. He read that Aunt Sue's brother Hal, would be given a small stipend of $10,000 yearly for the rest of his life and that Wanda, Tony and Carry would share in this gift if he so chose. The Chadworths shrieked in outrage and demanded to know what the meaning of this silliness was. Did she leave her estate to charity? Mr. Severied peered over his glasses at me and said no, that the entire remains of Aunt Sue's fortune and Rigby House in its entirety were left to **Lady Timothea Claire Chadworth Tottersham**. A stunned silence filled the room before pandemonium broke out. The entire family was screeching and crying. Uncle Hal asked furiously who Lady Timothea Claire Chadworth Tottersham was. I sat in a stunned silence as Mr. Severied explained that I was the sole heir to Aunt Sue's wealth as her only child. He stated that any further explanation would be for me to tell if I chose and it would all be made clear to me in private. He asked me to stay and thanked everyone else for coming. My family was screaming that I was a scheming little upstart and this wouldn't be the last of it and slammed out the door. Mary and Perry rushed over to me and gave me a big hug, and left quietly saying they would see me back at the house.

I continued to sit in stunned silence and listened while Mr. Severied told me of my background that had brought me to this unexpected place in my life.

"I am afraid it is a long and dangerous journey that your Aunt Sue, uh, mother traveled," he said. "I have known her for years and she entrusted me with her secret. We devised a plan to keep you safe at all cost. She would be able to see you and let you know her a little bit. She would go in her study and cry when she saw you after a long absence, but she had to remain aloof to your presence. She was so proud of you, but could only let you know in a cursory way. I was with her when she gave birth and she dared to keep you for only two days—she poured a vast amount of love into that time. And then I took you to Wanda.

We knew money would be an incentive and if Wanda had not wished to keep you we would have come up with another way. That tells you how it came about for you to be left with Wanda. I drew up the contract and Wanda and Hal had to agree to keep you until you could fend for yourself. They were well paid for the privilege of keeping Sue's little darling. Money has never been an object as Sue was a talented and gifted writer. Over the years she has written and published under many different names and has amassed a large fortune in her own right as well as the money she received when your father was killed. He was murdered by someone who wanted his title and place in the world. No one knew he had an heir. Your mother was given a certain amount of money, and of course her title, to go away and never return or she would face certain death as your father had. Going to the authorities was not an option, as she was a commoner and a foreigner. She left the country where she had been so happy with her wonderful husband and returned to the United States. Her whirlwind romance with her handsome marquis, and subsequent marriage against all royal protocol, had caused a stir in the kingdom and she was alone and heartbroken. Without her beloved Tim she just left and came to me. I handled her legal affairs and she received a very handsome settlement from Tim's successor as well as the right to call herself the Dowager Marchioness. She did not know you were with her until several months had passed and we had to scramble to keep your life a secret. You would have been very much a threat to the present Marquis of Tottersham. She kept a constant vigil to be sure no one in Tottersham ever knew of you. Upon her death, or when you reached the age of twenty five, you were to be told and warned to watch for danger, and to receive your rightful title and inheritance. I fear someone knows you exist and are close to receiving that inheritance and had to do something about it. You are in dreadful danger through no fault of your own."

I was relieved that someone else thought that Aunt Sue was murdered. It was hard to think of her as my mother. We determined to work together and find her killer and bring him or her to justice. He told me there had to be an autopsy as she was alone when she died and she hadn't seen a doctor for several months. He said there would be no service as that is the way Sue wanted it.

Chapter 3

I pulled my little car onto the circular drive and sat looking at the house. I thought of the happy times I had had here and the feeling of welcome I had always felt when I arrived. The feeling was still with me even with the disturbance of the bushes and brick path directly under the cupola. My eyes followed the trajectory path from the roof to the brick walkway that circled the house. "I will find out who did this, Mother," I said to myself. I had gone straight to my little house for clothes and then to the library to arrange a couple of days off.

The front door opened and Mary and Perry stepped out onto the steps. Mary's eyes were red from crying and I felt grateful that someone had cared enough to cry for my mother. Perry was looking very upset. I went up to them and gave each of them a brief hug and we silently entered the house. Nothing much had changed in all the time I had been coming here and I felt the house surround me with peace.

"I have a meal prepared for you and I will serve it to you in the dining room, my lady," Mary said. I stiffened. "Mary, please, I am simply Thea and you must remember that. I am a stranger to myself and need to be treated as though nothing has changed. I hope you and Perry will continue to keep everything as Aunt Sue, I mean my mother, would have liked. Let's all go into the kitchen and eat just like we used to. I need time to adjust and need some normalcy. Let's talk of old times."

Perry cleared his throat. "We would like you to know that if it is satisfactory to you, Thea, we would like to continue in your employ, as Ms. Chadworth suggested. We have been here so long we know no other way. We are grateful for our mention in her will at all." My eyes filled with tears and I told them I was happy to hear that.

We had a very nice meal of cold cuts and salad and I helped Mary wash up after lunch, just like in the old days. All three of us made a great effort to be casual.

"I know you must want to know what I am going to do about everything, but I am very up in the air right now. I need to think about who I am, what I want to do, and how I will do it. Let's just go on as if nothing has happened and we can go from there. I have my job to consider and my house. I am so tired. I want to roam the house and rest."

I left the kitchen and immediately went to the third floor and climbed the stairs to the cupola. This really was the same as always as nobody but I ever came here except Mary to dust. I looked at the view of the cove through the large window that opened out for air when it became stuffy. There was a little walkway and rail that ran completely around the cupola. Aunt Sue had forbidden me to ever walk there and I obeyed her. She said she never went to the roof because she was terrified of heights and the thought of falling. I on the other hand loved the whole idea of a widow walking round and round the cupola watching for her husband's ship to come into the cove. The widow's walk and cupola had always been kept in excellent repair as had the rest of the great three-story house. Sue had purchased this house many years ago when her books had started to sell and she became very well-to-do. Wanda had almost hated her for her wealth, and the whole family had resented her fortune. I was the only one who loved to come here and always felt close to her even if she was sometimes very standoffish and quiet.

The invitation to stay was always open to the whole family, but I was the only one who stayed as much as I could.

Now the tears I had been holding back came and I sobbed my heart out. I cried for Aunt Sue and I cried for myself, as I would never know her as my mother. I knew she had not fallen from the widow's walk because she never in a million years would have been up here. Someone had either brought her here and pushed her or had killed her and then threw her off the walk. I needed to find out. I was determined to talk with the police and find out exactly what happened. I knew that Mary and Perry had been away from the house on their holiday and she was supposed to be alone. She was quite capable of fending for herself when they took their time off several times a year, Mary to visit friends in Boston and Perry to check in on his mother every couple of months. They were due home that same day and Perry found her on the brick pathway when he returned. Mary returned to a house swarming with police and chaos.

Chapter 4

I left the roof and went down to Mother's study. This door had always been locked and I was surprised to find it open. Her study was in perfect order and looked as if someone had recently tidied up her desk and files. I began to scout among her things and it became apparent after a few minutes that there was nothing in the study to warrant its being closed. It didn't look much like the place a writer would come to work—no unfinished manuscripts or computer. It looked more like an office that was waiting for a new employee to put down his or her stuff. I was furious. I rushed to the kitchen to talk with Mary. I found her peeling vegetables for supper. "What happened to Mother's study? Why is the door open? What happened to all her writing stuff? Who cleaned it out and tidied up in there?"

"That is the way I found it when I came back from vacation, dear. I can only guess that Ms. Sue didn't lock it when she was alone. I thought maybe the police had taken anything they might have thought of interest. I don't know what was in there as I had never been in there in all the years I have been here. I did think it rather odd. Why would Ms. Sue lock that room? There is nothing there that looks like a secret to me. I'm sorry you are upset, Thea. Why don't you call the police department and talk with them? Perhaps they will return anything that they removed." I left the kitchen and returned to the study. I picked up the directory and looked up the non-emergency number for the sheriff's department. They said they would have somebody call me back. I sat there in my mother's chair trying to get some vibes from her. "What could I do? How should I start?" I was totally at a loss. I went back outside and again looked at the roof of the house. I was more convinced than ever that Mother had been murdered. I looked out on the bay. It was completely isolated here. Unless someone had been out there in a boat, it was impossible to find anyone that might have seen something. I went back into the house and up to the room I had always used when I visited. It was exactly the same. I stretched out on the bed and fell into a deep sleep. I dreamed.

I saw Mother walking on a beach. She was happy. She was young and her long blond hair was blowing out behind her. She had always worn her hair in a neat twist at the back of her head and I had never seen her with her hair down. I wore my own hair the same way. She was with a man. He was tall and handsome. He looked like . . . me. His rather longish hair was the same rich auburn as mine. He had his head thrown back and was laughing.

I woke with a start. Mary was standing in the doorway telling me supper was ready. I made a quick stop in Mother's room after washing up in my bathroom. There was nothing there to indicate that she had ever existed. I went down to the kitchen to share a meal with Mary and Perry. I asked them if they had ever seen any pictures in Mother's room. "No dear," Mary said. "I never saw any personal items in her room. I always thought she had it all in her study to keep her company."

Perry said, "She sure was a private person, Miss, nothing wrong with that of course. I asked her once if she wanted me to get her a pet and she said, 'I don't want anything to get all sentimental about Perry.' She did enjoy preparing for the Christmas times with your family, though—she would shop and hum carols for weeks. Then as soon as you had all left, she would become her own quiet self again."

I went back to my room and waited in vain for the phone call from the police. I fell asleep reading a book I had brought with me from the library. I didn't dream again.

Chapter 5

The police arrived the next morning as I was finishing a light breakfast. I sat admiring the beautiful room. I should say rooms, as the kitchen was really kind of a suite. The main kitchen was modernized old fashion. By that, I mean it was modern without compromising the elegance of the old house, the large pantry, the huge fireplace hearth, and an alcove that looked out on the cove with a table and chairs.

I saw the police car arrive and a large man stepped out and looked around. He looked up at the roof and down to the brick walkway, pretty much as I had yesterday. From where I sat in the alcove, I could see he was young, maybe in his early thirties. He didn't have a hat on and his light blond hair was very curly and rather long for a police officer. It curled onto his neck and actually looked tidy and neat. He was dressed in a brown sheriff's uniform that hugged his trim body in a very nice way. He moved with the grace of a much smaller man. I quickly went to the kitchen door and asked him in. I blushed when I realized he might think I was bringing him through the hired help entrance. "I am just eating my breakfast, would you care to join me?" I asked quickly.

"Perhaps a cup of coffee," he said in a beautiful baritone voice. Mary soon had him fixed up with a cup of black coffee and said, "I'll get started on the laundry if you don't need anything else, Thea." She left us sitting at the table and went about her chores.

"My name is Lieutenant Clark Sanderson of the sheriff's department," he said. "I understand you have some questions about your aunt's death." He looked at me with sharp, deep blue eyes that seemed very suspicious. I gazed back at him in my calm way that my friend Emmy said was my "Miss Librarian look".

"I am Thea Chadworth and Sue Chadworth was my mother," I said. He gave a start and pulled a notebook out of his pocket.

"It says here that Ms. Chadworth had no family except her brother and his family. Please explain, Ms. Chadworth."

"Thea, please," I said. "I am sure it sounds strange to you, but I just found out that Sue Chadworth was my mother. She had reasons to keep it a secret and I never knew. I was led to believe I was an orphan and left on the proverbial doorstep of Hal and Wanda Chadworth. I have a few questions about my mother's death, yes."

Lieutenant Sanderson said, "Hey, slow down, let's start from the beginning. I have been looking at this case since I returned from vacation and have some questions of my own. Who stands to inherit this substantial estate? I think there are some loose ends that need to be tied up here."

"I am her sole heir, except for a few small bequests to her employees and her brother. It was a total shock to all of us."

"Did anyone expect to inherit her fortune? Did her brother think he would inherit?" he asked. "When did you find out you were the heir? I need some answers. I feel this whole case needs to be reopened. That might bring your inheritance into question."

I stared at him in wonder. He was telling me he thought my mother's death was suspicious and I was totally surprised.

"Does that shock you, Ms. Chadworth?" he asked. "If you knew you were to inherit, that would give you a motive for Sue Chadworth's death."

I gurgled with laughter. "I am delighted you suspect me, Lieutenant. I thought I would have the devil of a time convincing you that my mother was murdered. Believe me, I don't think this is funny for a minute, but the irony of the situation makes me laugh. My attorney, Mr. Severied, will explain how my unusual situation came about, with my permission. We want whoever did this monstrous killing to be brought to justice. We will do everything in our power to help you."

Lieutenant Sanderson sat and looked at me. "What makes you think she was murdered? My team closed out this case as an accident while I was on vacation."

"Your team did not know that my mother would not have been on that widow's walk in a million years, if she was alive. She was totally freaked out by heights and forbade me to open the big double-hung windows if I intended to step out onto the walkway. I could open it for fresh air, but that was it. If she thought I had ever gone out on the walkway she would have banned the cupola as off limits and it was my favorite place in the house. She always had a workman come in once a year to insure all of the roof and cupola were safe. You can imagine I was tempted, but I was so grateful for the peace that I felt there I never gave in to temptation. You can see for miles up there and the cove is so beautiful no matter the season or the weather. She would not have been there, period. She said she could see all she needed to see by sitting on the front porch. Mr. Severied and I agree that she wouldn't have been on the walkway while she was alive."

"Can you show me the cupola now? I would like to reprocess the scene. I am sorry that this has taken so long to be investigated properly, but nobody mentioned her fear of the roof before. I imagine that since she was supposed to be alone when she died that the question was never asked. I'd also like to interview your employees again if I might."

I immediately rose from my chair and we went to the third floor. I led him up the stairs to the tower room with the cupola and he gasped at the beauty when he walked into the room.

"I guess there is no sense in fingerprinting the window now. It looks like the room has been thoroughly cleaned recently." He crossed to the heavy double-hung casement windows that opened out onto the walkway and opened them. He stepped out onto the walkway and to my amazement turned and offered me his hand.

"I don't imagine Ms. Chadworth can banish you to the parlor now. I will stay next to you if you have no head for heights."

I grasped his hand and scrambled out the door after him. I just stood and realized a childhood dream of going through the window door and actually standing on the walkway. We turned as one and started to walk around the outside of the tower and cupola. It was grand! I must have been beaming with joy, for he looked at me strangely and continued to walk.

"I always felt sorry for Aunt Sue, that she was afraid to come here. To me it was the best thing in my life. I can only hope she was dead when she was brought to the roof, for she would have been so terrified." Tears started to run down my face and I was embarrassed. I brushed them quickly away and when we arrived at the doorway again Lieutenant Sanderson assisted me into the room. We crossed to the reading chairs that were placed under the windows on the west side of the cupola. There was a book on the table between the chairs—*Little Women* by Louisa May Alcott. It was one of my favorite books and I had left it there the last time I was home. Funny, how I always thought of this big house on Rigby Cove as home.

When I stopped reminiscing and looked at Lieutenant Sanderson he was watching me closely with those dark blue eyes.

"You must have been surprised to learn that Ms. Chadworth was your mother," he said. "It must have come as a total shock."

"When I was small, I used to come here and fantasize about Sue being my real mother. I loved everything about the place. She taught me how to use the little skiff and sailboat in the boathouse and we would sometimes have a picnic on the sand. Sometimes we would take the large cabin cruiser and go across to Ellie's Island. I was never happier, and I thought she looked happy at those times too. Then she would withdraw into herself again and close the study door with her behind it. Nobody was allowed into her sanctum and the door was always kept locked." I suddenly remembered and turned to him with a question. "Does the police department have the stuff that was taken from the study?"

"Nothing was taken from the premises," he said. "There was no reason to think the study had anything to do with the accident. The house was clean and empty. No locked doors or suspicious activity anywhere. Just what seemed a terrible accident, and my team deemed it as such. I wanted a closer look after reading the report and I am glad I did. However; I think you would have quickly brought it to my attention had I not. The amount of your mother's estate is what waved a red flag as well."

"I never thought of Aunt Sue as rich. I just knew she didn't work away from home and she was very generous to the Chadworths and I was included. I was three when we first were invited for the holidays and I thought I had died and gone to heaven. Even though Aunt Sue was very distant to me I felt closer to her than I did to the others. They always treated me well, but I never knew love. The feeling I got when I was around Sue made me feel warm and comforted as if I had been here before. When an invitation was extended to us children for summer vacation, the others whined that they didn't want to leave their friends. Even though I was only three I knew I wanted as much of this place as I could get. I was not a child who asked for anything that wasn't offered, but I wanted to come back so bad, I asked if I could. Aunt Wanda saw a chance to get a rest from me for a while and Aunt Sue off-handedly said that I wouldn't be much of a bother so it was agreed. I came every time it was offered and it was offered to me almost as an open invitation. Wanda would arrange it as often as she dared without taking advantage of Sue and I sure didn't complain about being shipped to Rigby House. Aunt Sue would take me out on the water and she taught me to use the boats and to paint with oils and watercolors. I would find new toys and books each time I came and you can imagine for someone starved for affection I thought I was the luckiest girl in the world. I thought Carry and Tony were missing so much by not coming, but they said Aunt Sue was a cold fish. I just never got that feeling from her."

I told Lieutenant Sanderson all about being found on the doorstep and the written guarantee of money to raise me. I told of going to college, my degree in library science, my house, car and friends. I talked of how much I loved books and the library and what I had done to improve and expand it. He just sat and let me talk until I ran down in embarrassment. He knew more about me in that hour than anyone else, except my friend Emily Harrison with whom I had a lot in common. She was my assistant at the library and I had left her in charge until I decided what I wanted to do. I also told him of what Mr. Severied had informed me about my father's death and his title, and of my mother's return in fear for her own life and mine when she found out I was imminent.

"I am so sorry. I don't know what came over me. To sit here in what I call my room with another person for the first time just opened the floodgates. Please forgive me."

Lieutenant Sanderson turned to look at me. He had been watching the water and listening with a quiet intensity and I felt very calm in his presence.

"You have given me a lot to think about. I have a few things to check out and I will get back to you in a couple of days. Did the housekeeper and gardener tell you anything about what happened?"

I told him what Mary and Perry had said about finding her and how the study was open and empty of all personal items, and what they knew of her personality and life for the time they had been here. I told him of the clause for them in the will and how shocked everyone was to find that I had a title and was the heiress.

"I would like to speak to them before I leave. I have some additional questions. Do you feel safe here?" he asked.

"Yes, I am sure no one would come around with Perry on the premises. The Chadworths were very angry about the will, but I am not worried that they will harm me. I don't know about the harm my mother feared for me. I guess I will have to wait and see. I will show you back to Mary."

We returned to the kitchen after detouring to my mother's room for a quick inspection by the lieutenant.

Mary and Perry were having coffee and stopped talking when they heard us approaching. I'm sure they were speculating why we had been in the cupola so long. Perry gave me a quick glance.

"Is it necessary to put Thea through all of this? She has had a terrible time of it. Why can't you leave her alone?"

"It's alright Perry, I asked the lieutenant to look into Mother's death. I feel she was murdered and he is trying to put the facts together. Please help him in any way that you can."

Perry and Mary gasped. The color drained from their faces.

"Murdered!" Mary squeaked. "Why do you think she was murdered, Thea? I thought it was an awful accident. I'm sure you are just upset over Ms. Sue's death, Thea. Believe me it was just a tragedy and you will come to see that when you think about it," Mary said.

"I will never change my mind, Mary. My mother would have never gone to the cupola. You know that as well as I do—she was terrified of heights."

"I'm sorry, Thea, we know she was afraid of the cupola room, but we were just talking about the possibility that she had cleaned out her room and study and had decided to jump from the roof. That would explain everything. She might have decided to do it while we were all gone. She was a very secretive woman. Maybe she was more troubled than we knew," Mary said.

I exchanged a glance with Lieutenant Sanderson and quietly left the room. A little while later I watched Lieutenant Sanderson from the cupola walkway as he went to the dock and looked over the cove. He went to the boathouse and checked out the little skiff and larger cabin cruiser and sailboat. Mother had been an avid sailor and Perry used the boats and kept them totally seaworthy. I had gone fishing with him many times in my youth and he was always very patient with me. I appreciated that Perry and Mary might think mother had committed suicide, but I didn't think for one moment that she had. I remembered the glance I had shared with Lieutenant Sanderson and felt that he didn't think so either. As he came back up the pathway from the dock, he looked up and gave me a small salute when he saw me on the walkway. His way of saying good for you I guess. I waved back and he folded his large frame into his cruiser and slowly drove around the circular drive and out onto the roadway. We both had a lot to think about.

Chapter 6

Clark Sanderson did have a lot to think about and he was becoming surer all the time that Susan Chadworth had not killed herself. Mary and Perry didn't have much to add to their theory that she had disposed of all personal material and then climbed to the roof to jump. Clark felt she would know that falling from that height might not kill her and she would be maimed for life. He was sure she was dead before she even got to the roof and now he had to prove it. He headed into Rigby to talk with Mr. Severied. The medical examiner would have to take another look at the body, too.

Several hours later as I was changing to drive to Trafton to see Emmy and make arrangements for a long-term absence from the library, I remembered the key to Sue's safe deposit box. Mr. Severied had given it to me as I was leaving his office. He said he did not know what it contained, but thought I should look into it as soon as possible. I decided to stop at the bank on my way out of Rigby. I gathered the proof of ownership that Mr. Severied had given me along with the key, and left through the front door. Perry was standing on the front steps and was startled when I appeared. He looked sad.

"I am going to Trafton for the afternoon and should be back in time for supper. Please let Mary know." He looked closely at me and said he would. I saw him looking after me as I circled the drive and drove in the same direction Lieutenant Sanderson had taken.

The bank was just down the street from Mr. Severied's office and I wasn't surprised to see Lieutenant Sanderson's vehicle parked in front of the office. I went into the bank and asked to speak with the bank manager. Her name was Marion Reed and she had known Aunt Sue. She was more than glad to help me and gave me her condolences about my aunt. She didn't know Sue was my mother and I didn't tell her. After assuring that I was indeed the owner of the box, she opened the bank's side and left me to use my key on the other side. I was alone in the huge vault room and felt very nervous about what I would find. I opened the very large box. It was one of the largest in the vault and I couldn't imagine what was in it.

The first thing I saw was a picture of me in my graduation gown from college. She had had it enlarged and framed. I noticed right away that there were many pictures of me at different times in my life, from infant to high school graduation. She had pictures of me in the boat and on the lawn, playing croquet, with Mary and Perry. One of them was of me reading a favorite book in the library. I cried as I thought of her taking pictures of her child from a distance to look at when she was alone. My original birth certificate in an ornate envelope was there as well as a copy of the one I had grown up with. There were no names submitted on the parents' lines of the ones I had lived under, just "unknown," but my original had all the information of my real mother and father. There was quite a bit of money in cash, for emergencies I surmised, as there was several hundred thousand at a glance. Near the bottom of the box was a large framed picture of a man—the same man I had seen with her on the beach in my dream. She had a small picture of me tucked into the bottom of the frame. There was no mistaking the resemblance. A small sticky note stuck to the frame next to my picture said "Our beautiful daughter my darling". Under the picture were about eight very thick envelopes, the kind you might find a manuscript in. I pulled out the envelopes and saw that they were numbered and dated, starting about a year before my birth. There was also a very elegant jewelry box that contained the most beautiful jewelry I had ever seen. There was a piece for every occasion you could imagine.

The manager gladly supplied me with a carton that was large enough to contain all the contents of the deposit box and also allowed me to close the flap and secure it. The money I left in the safety deposit box after counting it. There was $500,000 in cash. I also left the jewelry box. I was nervous about taking the contents from the bank as Mother must have thought they needed to stay here, but I took the carton and placed it in the back seat of my little car and drove to Trafton to see Emmy.

"Boy, am I glad to see you!" she said. "I thought we had lost you." She was very busy and I helped her out for a few minutes. When we had caught up with the rush, I explained that I would hire someone to help her out as I was going to have to take some time off and she would be in charge until I returned.

"Oh, Thea, can I do that? If I have to work with someone I would like to be the one to hire them. It would help you out too and I actually have someone in mind. You remember Temple Mathieu, don't you? She went to school with us and took some of the same courses. She worked at the Gull Restaurant in the summer to put herself through school. She is a hard worker and loves the library profession."

"What a great idea, Em. Yes, I remember Temple. She will be terrific for the job. I will see that the board allows you to work at your own discretion. Since the library is endowed by Aunt Sue, I don't think there will be a problem, especially since I am now the benefactor."

"What!" squealed Emmy. "You definitely need to catch me up, girl." I told her what had transpired over the last couple of days, and she was more than glad to help in any way she could. She was shocked to find I thought Mother had been murdered and even more shocked to find out Sue was my mother.

"Lady Timothea," she joked "I will be so honored to assist you." I smacked her with a magazine and it felt good to be with someone I could talk to. I told her I had some treasures that I needed to keep in a safe place and be able to access them at a moment's notice. We agreed that the safe in the library would be perfect. It is huge and can only be opened with a combination. We brought the carton in from my locked VW and placed it in the safe. I kept out the envelope that was dated first of the series. I intended to read it and get it back here as soon as possible. I swore Emmy to secrecy and she was glad to be in on the investigation.

I called the board president, Andrea Collins, and explained that I was now the main supporter of the library with the death of my aunt and she fell all over herself to let Emmy take charge, not that she wouldn't agree anyway. She was a nice person and had known Sue. She expressed her sympathy and I hung up with a clear conscience to start on my hunt for my mother's killer. First, I needed to arm myself with some facts and I was pretty sure the manuscripts were a good place to start.

Chapter 7

Upon returning to Rigby Cove, I determined to hide the manuscript where no one could find it. I went to the third floor and started going from room to room. This floor of rooms was always clean, but never used for everyday living. Perry lived over the garage and Mary had her own little suite next to the kitchen, with its own entryway. The doors were all closed and the rooms neat and tidy. I needed to find somewhere that was easy to get to but hard to find. I had explored all of these rooms when I was a child and remembered a cubby behind a closet in the third room on the right. I opened the closet door and pushed on the panel to open the cubby. It was hard to open and when it finally gave I found out why. It was crammed from floor to ceiling with all of mother's personal belongings including her word processor and a picture of my father. I thought there must be several dozen manuscripts. Who would have put them here? It couldn't have been mother, she wouldn't have treated her manuscripts in this way, cramming them in like this, and my father's picture was in a frame with the glass cracked. No way.

I rushed to the phone in my room and put in a call to Lieutenant Sanderson. He had given me his personal number and he answered on the third ring. I told him what I had found and he said he would be right over. I went back to the third floor from my room on the second floor and sat on the stairs waiting, my numbered manuscript clutched in my hand.

It was about fifteen minutes when I heard a vehicle tear into the drive and another couple of minutes before I heard Mary puffing up the stairs behind Lieutenant Sanderson.

"That girl is breaking her heart over nothing. She has to forget this silliness, Lieutenant." He asked Mary politely to return to the kitchen as he spotted me sitting forlornly on the stairs.

"Show me where you found the stuff, Thea." He said. I got up off the stairs and he followed me to the third room on the right. I opened the door and showed him the cubby behind the closet. "She would have never crammed her personal stuff in here like this and look at my father's picture. She would never, ever break the glass or leave it this way. I know it must look like what Perry said is true, but she would have put this stuff with the other in her bank safety box. This was done in a hurry and someone must have known this cubby was here."

"I agree. Your mother had a safety box at the bank? Who would know this cubby was here, besides Mary and Perry?"

"Yes, after you left, I remembered that Mr. Severied had given me a key and papers of ownership when I was at the reading of the will. I went to the bank today and opened the box. There were all kinds of pictures of me as a child growing up and lots of money. There was also a bunch of manuscripts that are numbered and dated. I have the first one right here." I raised the envelope I had in my hand to show him. "I intend to read them one at a time. I have the others in a safe place. I will start to read this one tonight."

"Please let me know if you are given any clues to this mystery. I will take the items that will show fingerprints easily to be processed and return them to you tomorrow."

I went to the kitchen for a carton, and wearing gloves, he placed them carefully in the cruiser. Mary and Perry watched us. After he had gone they just went into the house and I went to the dock to think. "Who knew about the cubby?" I thought. "We have the heavy work cleaners and painters in all the time, but how would they know about the cubby? Did Mother have regular visitors, who would have used that room?" I needed to talk with Mary, now.

I found her in the kitchen stirring a sauce and she looked at me with weary eyes. "Please, Thea, let it go. We don't want to believe she killed herself either, but the stuff Lieutenant Sanderson took away must prove to you that she hid her personal stuff and then jumped off the roof." I put my arm around her and said, "I'm sorry Mary, I can't let it go. She was my mother and I missed so much of her in my life that I have to find out what happened to her. Please tell me what you know about visitors to the rooms on the third floor."

"She had her editors and proofreaders stay from time to time. Sometimes several people at once if she was close to publishing and they would party for a few days. They all stayed on the third floor and didn't ask for my help with cleaning or anything while they were here. There were quite a few of them, some the same and some different. She would only say these are my friends and how many would be staying over and how many we would be feeding, so I could shop. I'm afraid I don't remember their names. There were just a lot at times and then she wouldn't see anyone for months. She never scheduled any of these people when you were coming. I don't think she wanted to expose you to that type of people. Pardon me, but they were kind of brash and you were so gentle."

"Thank you, Mary. Please trust me in this—I know some things that you don't and I am positive my mother was killed. If you can think of anything that she might have been afraid of or anyone, please let me know."

Chapter 8

Several days later I was in the front hall. I had moped and mourned and was now ready to do something. Perry must have been down to the mailbox, as there was a pile of mail on the stand by the front door. I picked up the pile and began to sort through it. There were several checks from different publishers and I began to think I might be able to track down through these checks some of the people that Mary talked about. I had taken another carton and gone to the third floor after the lieutenant had left the other day. I had placed everything that Lieutenant Sanderson didn't take with him in the carton and put it on a chair in my mother's study. I left the carton on the chair and started to go through the mail. There was a cream-colored envelope made from expensive velum and it was addressed to me. I opened it with trepidation and found it to be an invitation to a reception for Senator Frank Vermillion in Trafton. The invitation was at the express request of Arabella Vermillion, his wife. She sent a note asking me to please attend as it would be a good way to be introduced into Sue's society. She expressed hers and the senator's deepest regret for what happened to Sue. She said to bring a guest as it would make me feel more at ease with strangers. She said it was white tie and hoped I would consider giving her a call to accept her invitation. The reception would be at their home on Saturday evening starting at eight o'clock. She left her private number.

I called a locksmith and asked him to please make it today and I would pay him for his inconvenience. He agreed to be there at three. I spent the next two hours trying to sort through some of the papers that were taken from the closet. I was making a list of Mother's contacts in the publishing world and was amazed at the list of people that was mounting up. I thought Lieutenant Sanderson would be pleased with me for my list of suspects. I was determined to talk with these people as soon as possible. I still hadn't read whatever was in my numbered envelope, but was keeping it close to my side and wanted to get to it as soon as I could. I had been listless for several days but now I was determined to buckle down and do what needed to be done. I felt that I might possibly get some clues from anyone at the reception who might have known Mother well. I had heard of these people of course— I had grown up in Trafton after all. They were considered high society by Aunt Wanda and she would give her eye teeth to be one of them.

I called Emmy and she said she was attending also with Bruce Garrett, her boyfriend. Emmy's family was from this level of society but you would never know it. I said I would have to think about it and she said to come as we would have great fun.

As I settled back in Mother's chair, the locksmith arrived and Mary showed him in with a hurt look on her face. I told him what I wanted and in an hour's time there was a beautiful new lock on the study door. I retained the only key and added it to a favorite locket Aunt Sue had given me for my tenth Christmas with her. I always wear it. I just love it. It has an odd design and no pictures inside, but I still love it because she gave it to me. I clipped the key on the chain for easy access and closed the door. As I stepped into the hall, the front doorbell rang. It was Lieutenant Sanderson with the articles he had taken with him.

"There were no prints on anything here, except inside the glass on your father's picture. Those of course were your mother's. We obtained them when she was killed." He was apologetic about mentioning something that was done to her body. I opened up the new lock with the key I unclipped from my locket, and we placed the carton he had brought with him on the desk. I looked at the picture of my father and found that he had replaced the glass. "Thank you," I said as my eyes met his.

I told him what Mary said about the visitors and showed him my list and the checks that had come in the mail. He was surprised at my progress and said so.

His eyes fell on the velum envelope on the desk with the return address. "My, my you are treading in high society Lady Tottersham. How did they find out you were royalty?"

My eyes flashed at his little joke. "They have no idea Sue was my mother. They are merely recognizing my wealth as her heir I imagine."

He grinned. "I imagine you are correct, nothing but the best for the senator and his wife." I opened the envelope and showed him the invitation. "Are you going?" he asked.

"I thought it would be a good way to speak to some people that knew mother on her own terms. I would go as her niece of course."

"I see you need an escort. I also have an invite and was not planning on attending, but would you do me the honor of attending with me? Hard telling what we might come up with."

I tried to check my surprise, but was unsuccessful and he laughed. "What? You didn't think a lowly cop would be invited?"

"I sincerely hope you don't think of me as that much of a snob. I was merely surprised that you wanted to attend with me. I thought you might have someone else to take."

"I can assure you, this is strictly business and we can work together to get some answers. I'll pick you up at seven thirty Saturday evening. I will take your list to work on in the meantime. Do you have a copier?" I made him a copy and his amused look preceded him out the door.

Now, to make peace with Mary and Perry. Supper was just being put on the table when I entered the kitchen. Mary glanced at me with the hurt look still on her face. Perry was washing up in the laundry room. "Mary, please don't take offense at my putting a new lock on the study door. I am trying to get back to the place where Aunt Sue, I mean, Mother was. I want things to be the same. It is important to me to have a private place. I hope you understand. It has nothing to do with you or Perry, but someone entered this house once before and I want to be sure they can't mess with my papers again." She grumbled, "I think you are making this harder than necessary on yourself, Thea, but this is your house and we will abide by your wishes." We sat down at the table and to my surprise; Mary bowed her head and said grace for the first time in a long time. It felt good to me and I said "Amen." I helped her clean up after a scrumptious meal and dessert. Things were good with us once more. I went to the study and started to read my numbered manuscript.

Chapter 9

My name is Dola Fields and I am a romance author. I have written many novels and have traveled the world doing research.

My name is Peter Trapton and I am a spy thriller author. I have written many novels and have traveled the world doing research.

My name is Grace Pelton and I write murder mysteries. I have written many novels and have traveled the world doing research.

My name is Grant Sabold and I write an adventure series. I have traveled the world doing research.

My name is Karen Fulsom and I am a romance author. I have traveled the world doing research.

My name is Trudy Chever and I write mysteries. I have traveled the world doing research for my novels.

My name is Susan Chadworth and no book I have ever written could be more complicated or adventurous than my own story. This is my story.

I arrived in London tired and grumpy from jet lag. I had been traveling for days and I had to see one of my editors and wasn't looking forward to it. I came through the turnstile and promptly dropped one of the two briefcases I was carrying. In spite of its being locked, it hit a corner of the walkway just right and burst open, scattering my latest Peter Trapton novel and various writing utensils across my feet. A well-kept hand reached down and picked up my manuscript. The hand belonged to my future. The man who straightened his long body to a standing position was looking at the title cover of my manuscript and then stared at me with fascinating eyes. They were the color of green glass and went strikingly with his longish dark auburn wavy hair. He was very tall and I had to look up to meet his gaze. "Surely you are not Peter Trapton, a woman as beautiful as you could not possibly get Giles into so many fixes."

"All right, if you say so, I am not Peter Trapton." He grinned at me and said, "Please, Peter let me take my favorite author to lunch. I have had a rotten week and it would go some way to helping me out of my funk. Allow me to introduce myself, I am Tim Tottersham."

His British accent was posh and he was obviously well-to-do. I didn't usually allow myself to be picked up at airports by handsome men but this fellow had to be the exception.

He steered me to a waiting vehicle and the driver loaded my luggage along with his into the boot of the car. We dined at a fancy restaurant. The maitre d' obviously recognized him and we were seated at a private table in an alcove. We spent three hours talking Giles out of different situations and when I looked at my watch I was stunned that so much time had elapsed. His car was waiting and the driver held the door and said, "Where to, my lord?" I stopped halfway in the car and looked back at him. He took his time taking his eyes off my bum and grinned at me. "It seems that both of us have an alias my love. Now don't go all stuffy on me. I would like to spend more time with you as my funk has totally fled. I will drop you at your appointment and you can call when you are ready to be picked up, no pun intended." He grinned again and folded himself into the car, which I now noted was a Bentley. The driver knew my editor's address and in a little while we were there. Tim stepped out of the car, kissed my hand, and jumped back into the vehicle like a kid and they sedately disappeared into London traffic. I tucked the number to his phone into my jacket pocket and, smiling, went in to see George, my London editor. It seemed I would have to call his lordship as he had quite sneakily driven off with my luggage in his car.

I found my business with George wasn't so tedious after all and we quickly finished what we had to do to promote my latest Lord Giles. How ironic that I had met the real Lord Giles long after my mind had created him.

"What do you know of Lord Tim Tottersham, George?"

"Well, from all reports he is a real stand-up guy. Very rich of course and from what I hear a favorite with his peers of the realm. He owns a very large estate just outside of London and he plays the field with the ladies. He is very popular. Mind your way with him Susan my dear. He is very much his father's son."

I thanked him for everything, said I would see him again and left his office. I stepped out onto the sidewalk and there was Lord Tottersham's vehicle blithely blocking traffic. He jumped out before his driver could and held the door for me. I climbed into the Bentley and Tim said "Home James" with a grin.

Chapter 10

The phone rang just as I decided to go down for supper. "Hi, Thea," Emmy said. "I was thinking that you will need to come into Trafton to your house to get an outfit for Saturday. Do you want to meet there for a consultation? We haven't had an event to dress formal for in quite a while. I know you have some scrumptious gowns and we will have a ball deciding what we want to wear."

"Sure, I am just going down to supper and I will meet you there at seven o'clock. I have a couple of dresses that I got a while ago, just in case I met that certain someone." I laughed. "You will know more about what would be appropriate for that type of occasion. See you there."

I left shortly after supper and as Perry had put the VW in the four-car garage, I decided to take Mother's Jaguar. It was a silver convertible and really pretty. Perry uses the SUV and Mary always drives the wagon for shopping. I don't know why I decided to use the fancy car, I just did. I drove out of the garage and circled down the drive toward Trafton. One must go through Rigby to get to Trafton which is about ten miles west of Rigby, and Rigby is five miles from Rigby Cove. It was a nice warm spring day and I decided to keep the top down. I tooled along about forty-five miles an hour. I have never been a fast driver, and Mother used to tease me about being so staid while driving as she really liked speed, thus the Jaguar. I laughed to myself and said to myself, "This car is really wasted on you, my friend." Up ahead a truck pulled out in front of me and because I am a very cautious driver I stepped on the brake to slow down. The brake went right to the floor and I thought, "Oh boy, here we go." There was a field on each side of the truck and I didn't hesitate to drive into the field on my side of the road. The Jaguar plowed up quite a bit of grass and dirt, but settled in the field, stuck in dirt, about forty feet along the side of the road in the field. I was shaken up, but thanks to my seatbelt I was okay. The truck driver was surprised to see me drive through the field on his right, and immediately stopped and ran over to see if I was all right. I told him I had lost my brakes and he turned white.

"Lady, this must be your lucky day. That grade a mile ahead of us leads to Dead Man's Curve and you would have been a goner. I was sorry I pulled out in front of you when I noticed you too late, but now I am glad. You would have been dead. Don't you ever service a nice car like that?"

"This was my aunt's car and the first time I have driven it in a long time. Thank you for your help and yes, saving my life."

He waited until I had called a tow truck and asked if I wanted him to stay with me as it was getting dark. "No, I am going to call a friend, thank you."

He went back to his truck and pulled away, and I picked my cell phone out of my purse. I dialed Lieutenant Sanderson's private number and he answered on the second ring. I told him what had happened. "I will be right there. Don't move the car until I get there. Tell Freddie to stay with you if he beats me there—I will need him."

I sat in the car thinking about what had just happened. This car was Mother's exclusive car. She hardly ever drove anything else. She drove fast. Her killer wasn't taking any chances, he wanted her dead. What could this mean? Who would have access to the Jaguar? Was it rigged? Freddie's Wrecker Service pulled over to the side of the road and a man looked out at the Jaguar. "What are you doing out there little lady, and why are you driving Sue Chadworth's Jag?"

I stepped out of the car. "My Aunt Sue has died and this is now my car, such as it is. I lost the brakes when a truck pulled out in front of me from that farm road back there." He started to speak and I said, "I know, I know, I just missed Dead Man's Curve up ahead."

"I didn't know Sue had died—what happened? No funeral? She kept that car in tip top shape. I know she did, I serviced it myself."

"She was killed a week ago and she didn't want a service. She will be buried with no fanfare, not even family attending. I, of course will be at her interment. Her lawyer was instructed to handle it that way. She fell off the roof of her house."

"No way, everybody knows Sue was afraid of heights, why would she be on the roof?"

I was spared from answering his question by the arrival of Lieutenant Sanderson's screaming squad car. He crossed to where we were standing in the early grass.

"Howdy Clark, what's going on anyway? This little lady tells me Sue fell off her roof and I know she wouldn't be up there in the first place and now I find out the brakes on her car quit. I checked that car just last month. There was nothing wrong with the brakes."

"Freddie, do me a favor and keep this under your hat, okay? I want you to check out this car from top to bottom for me. How do you plan to get it out of the field?"

"Well, this little lady's sharp driving followed right along the roadway so I think I can just winch it out." He pulled into the farm road and turned around. He pulled right up next to the field and just ahead of the Jaguar. Then he attached his cable to the front frame of the Jaguar and started his winch. The cable popped the car right out of the early grass and dirt in the field and after talking with Lieutenant Sanderson and repositioning the cable on the car he pulled it into the roadway and was off to his garage.

I looked at Lieutenant Sanderson. "Are we right, or are we right?"

"Little lady, I think we are right." I whacked him with my purse and he laughed.

"How do I get back to my place? Is there a taxi service here?"

"I will take you back; I want to have a look at your garage. Somebody had to have access to that car and I want to find out who."

"We don't lock the garage, but I guess we should, huh?"

"Yes, I guess you should."

While he drove back to Rigby Cove, I called Emmy and arranged to meet her later. When we arrived at Rigby Cove, Perry was inside the garage washing the cars. My little VW was immaculate. We got out of the cruiser and Perry rushed over to us.

"What happened?" he asked. "Where is the Jag?"

"The brakes failed on Ms. Chadworth's car and she was almost killed. We need to get to the bottom of whoever is doing this, Mr. Dawson. Who would have access to the cars in this garage besides you?"

"No one!" he shouted. "No one should be in my garage except me. Are you saying I would harm Thea?"

"I'm saying no such thing, Mr. Dawson. I'm asking who else could have had access to these vehicles."

"We don't lock the garage here, Lieutenant, so I guess just about anybody who wanted to sneak in here, but they don't want to have me catch them here."

"I want this garage locked immediately until I can check it out. I suppose you have already polished all of these vehicles?"

"I am sorry, yes sir. I like to keep busy and this is a good way to spend my time."

"I need to use my VW right away, Perry. Could you check the brakes and be sure it is fit to drive? I am already late for an appointment."

"I'll do it right away, Thea, but it will take a little while."

"Thanks Perry. Lieutenant, can I offer you a cup of coffee while I wait?"

"No, I think I will stay with Perry if you don't mind. I want to see how it is done. It might come in handy."

I went into the house and unlocked the study. I called Emmy and told her I would be along as soon as I could. I told her what had happened and she said, "Oh Thea, please be careful!"

Fifteen minutes later Perry told me my VW was ready and he said he would check all of the other vehicles too. Lieutenant Sanderson was standing by my VW parked in the drive and he opened the door for me. "I will follow you to your destination. Where are you going?"

"I am going to my house in Trafton. You don't have to follow me Lieutenant. I am sure I will be all right now."

"Let's go," he said.

I drove even slower into Trafton and I'm sure Lieutenant Sanderson regretted the offer to follow me, but we arrived at my little house safely. It was all lit up and he jumped out and asked who was in there. I laughed and told him Emmy had a key and was waiting for me to try on gowns. He frowned, said he would see me tomorrow night, added a good night, and left.

"Well, it must be nice to have your own escort. Do I detect a little romance?"

"Don't be silly, Em. He wanted to be sure the VW was all right."

"Let's get busy, I need my beauty sleep and your dress has to be perfect."

"Why are you so concerned, do you think I will embarrass you?"

"No, I have a very good reason why I want you to look perfect"

"What are you up to, Em? Let's see what I have got."

We went into my bedroom and opened the big walk-in closet. Emmy pushed through the dresses and stopped at a deep green form-fitting dress. It was one I had tried on when she was with me and I thought it was too daring, but she insisted I buy it. The dress was long and slit up the side to my thigh. It had a plunging neckline that required the wearer to go without a bra, but fit so nicely you really didn't need one. The dress was very elegant in spite of all its exposure and I had the perfect accessories to go with it. I had some really nice costume jewelry, and decided on some tinted pearls that matched the dress perfectly. Some nice mint green long elbow length gloves finished off the ensemble. I packed a couple of large bags and we locked up and left—happy little campers.

By the time I arrived back at Rigby Cove, it was late and after carrying in my dress and luggage I went straight to bed. Perry was up and put the VW in a locked garage.

The next day, I spent lots of time on me. I did want to look nice for the reception and worked on my appearance. I did my nails, both hands and toes, washed my hair, and took a long luxurious bath.

When I dressed for the party I looked in the mirror and thought, "I guess I won't embarrass Lieutenant Sanderson too badly."

The mirror showed a young woman with upswept glossy dark auburn hair, with a few curly tendrils around her face. The dress fit like a glove to a slim but rounded figure. She stood about five feet six in her beautiful dark green leather sandals. Her mint tinted pearls and matching earrings were just the right touch. Her dress color offset her creamy complexion and hair. She thought she would do. She was excited and her green eyes sparkled. She waited for the doorbell and when Mary let the Lieutenant in she was halfway down the stairs. He stepped into the hall and looked up at her. She caught her breath. He was dressed in an elegant tuxedo that showed off his physique and blonde good looks to the max. She continued down the stairs as he gazed at her. She hoped she wouldn't trip. Mary said, "Oh Thea, you are so beautiful! You will do us proud at the Vermillions' tonight."

Chapter 11

Clark Sanderson looked into Thea's beautiful green eyes and agreed with Mary. "You look very nice, we'd better hurry or we will be unfashionably late."

I held out my nicely gloved hand and he took my arm and walked me to a dark blue Mercedes parked at the door. I laughed. I couldn't help it, I felt like Cinderella.

"Care to share the joke?"

"I wondered if we would show up in a police cruiser."

He grinned and said, "This is my other car. You know as in 'My other car is a Mercedes.'"

"I got it," I said.

He helped me into the car and let his eyes linger on my silky thigh as I got in. I was carrying a matching wrap and I laid it on the seat between us. We were both silent as he drove off.

He talked about what he had found out from Freddie about the Jaguar. "The brake lines had been cut so that the first time the brakes were applied they would be useless."

I gasped. "I don't know why I am shocked, but just hearing it confirmed gives me the creeps." I grabbed my wrap and put it around my shoulders.

We arrived at the Vermillion mansion with time to spare and the valet took the Mercedes from Clark and we started to walk toward the door. I turned to him and said, "Thank you Lieutenant for escorting me and everything." He said, "Don't you think you should call me Clark? After all, we are supposed to be on a date."

"Clark it is. You should call me Thea."

I was very surprised when Clark opened the door and walked in without knocking, ushering me ahead of him. A woman with beautiful white hair set in Betty White style rushed forward to meet us. "Oh Clark, I am glad you are here. I was just going through."

"Mother, may I introduce you to Ms. Thea Chadworth? Thea, this is my mother, Sylvia Clark Sanderson."

The woman took my hand and said, "I am so glad to meet you, my dear. Let me introduce you around."

For the next half hour I was chaperoned around the room by Clark's mother with Clark bringing up the rear. The first people that the exuberant Sylvia met were Senator Frank Vermillion and his wife Arabella. Sylvia gave Clark no chance to introduce me to the couple but gushed out her own introduction. "Arabella and Frank, this is Thea Chadworth. Thea, this is Senator Frank and Arabella Vermillion. Thea, you will get to know them as Uncle Frank and Aunt Arabella. Arabella, as you have probably guessed this is Clark's new girlfriend."

I quickly looked at Clark and he had a grin on his face. I shot him a look and he laughed out loud. His mother quickly moved us on. I managed to stop long enough to put my wrap on a chair, and Clark slipped his arm around my shoulders. When I tried to extricate myself unobtrusively, he laughed and pulled me closer. Sylvia continued to whirl and Clark continued to grin so I joined the club. I put my arm around Clark's waist and snuggled down. He just chuckled.

Sylvia was wearing a beautiful designer gown of ice blue and it went very well with her dark blue eyes so much like her son's. Arabella was in a dark teal gown that screamed money and she wore her long blond hair down. I soon forgot most of the names that Sylvia hurled around, but I'm sure the whole room was aware of who I was by now.

We were approached by a handsome older man that looked like Clark. "Clark, I am probably the only person in the room who hasn't met your new friend."

"I am sorry, Dad. Thea this is my father, Granger Trafton Sanderson. Dad this is Thea Chadworth."

"I can see why my son is so quick to grab you up. Thea, please call me Granger. I will see you two later. We are at the same table."

Sylvia had buzzed off in another direction, having done her duty all around, leaving Clark to my mercy.

"Do you mind telling me what this is all about? Are you that desperate for a woman?"

"I didn't want you to come after me for my money," he laughed. I was about to bop him again when a beautiful woman in a red dress and long blonde hair came up to Clark and took him by the arm. "Clark, my darling, you are neglecting me something awful. People will begin to talk about us. Why don't we go get a drink?" She shot me a death glare and tried to pull Clark after her. He easily disengaged himself from her and said, "Hillary, you are being rude. Let me introduce you to my fiancée, Thea Chadworth. Thea, this is a childhood friend, Hillary Leighton. Thea and I are going to circulate now; we will probably see you later." I felt so sorry for Hillary as she stood with her face slowly turning a blotchy red.

"You were very mean to her and you are just getting us in deeper you know."

"She assumes way too much and needs to be put in her place. Let's get some investigating done." We did begin to talk with people about Sue Chadworth but nothing amounted to much.

We went in to dinner and were seated at the Senator's table. The table conversation was congenial and everyone was having a good time. Emmy had arrived with her parents and her fiancé Bruce Garrett and they were seated at the next table. I introduced Clark to Derrick and Hilda Harrison and Bruce and Clark were old friends.

When the band struck up a waltz, Clark stood and took my arm. He led me onto the floor and to my surprise he danced like a dream. We hardly left the floor for the rest of the night and I felt daggers being shot my way. When I glanced to the sideline Hillary was glaring for all she was worth. Emmy and I went to the powder room and Emmy said, "Boy, you've made a big enemy tonight. Nobody takes Hillary's man. Bruce said she was telling everyone they would be engaged tonight and he said Clark introduced you as his fiancée. I'd watch my back, Thea."

"Well, she will have to get in line. Someone else might beat her to it."

We went back to the ballroom and I saw that Hillary had wasted no time in moving in on Clark. They were dancing and she was trying to snuggle up to him. He stopped, said something to her, and escorted her off the floor. She fled to the powder room and smashed into me on the way. Granger happened to be standing right behind me and he steadied me on my feet and said, "That girl needs to be taught some manners. Clark made the mistake of being nice to her and she thought she could move in for the kill. My boy is too smart for the likes of that."

Clark joined us and asked, "Have you had enough, sweetheart?"

I said, "Yes, whenever you are ready, darling." Granger grinned and said good night. We found Sylvia and our hosts, the Vermillions, and bade them all good night. I went to the chair where I had dropped my wrap and gloves. When I picked them up I found that they had been cut to ribbons. Sylvia rushed over and exclaimed, "That nasty girl, how could she destroy something so nice? I hope you are through being nice to her, Clark. She is dangerous."

"We can't be sure she did it, Mom, but we'll keep that in mind."

We left the Vermillions' and while we waited for the valet to bring the Mercedes, Clark slipped off his jacket and put it around my shoulders. "I'm sorry, Thea. I will make it up to you." He pulled me close and bent his head. The kiss was soft and warm. I sighed and he deepened the kiss. We were interrupted by the valet and Clark muttered something under his breath.

We started the drive back to Rigby Cove. "Did you want to go to your house here in town?" he asked. I looked at him and was very tempted, but we had other fish to fry.

"Seriously, Thea, we had fun tonight standing the place on its ear, but you have to admit there is something between us. When this is all over I want to go somewhere with this relationship. You are the woman I have been waiting for and I intend to pursue you. Just giving you fair warning."

I didn't find it necessary to answer. I just nestled beneath his arm.

I felt kisses all over my face and opened my eyes. I had fallen asleep under his arm and he was kissing me awake. "Do you think you can wait for this case to come to its conclusion?" I asked.

"God knows I want to come in with you right now, but I have to keep my mind on keeping you safe. I will walk you in and see that all is okay."

We went to the door and I gave him the key. He unlocked the door and stepped into the hall. I followed him and gave him his jacket back. He put the jacket on and pulled the lapel toward his nose. "It smells like you." He pulled me into his arms and kissed me again. "I can't believe how you have knocked me right off my feet. I feel you are my destiny. Say you feel the same way."

"I feel the same way. I am so afraid I am dreaming and I will wake up and you will be stern Lieutenant Sanderson again."

"Stern Lieutenant Sanderson has to go get some rest and try to get you off my mind enough to sleep. I will see you tomorrow. Would you like me to come to brunch?"

I grinned. "Yes, please."

Chapter 12

I was too restless to settle and went into the study. I had put the locket and key in my purse for the evening and I now put them back on my neck as I removed the pearls. I picked up mother's manuscript and began reading.

It took an hour to get to Lord Tottersham's estate. It was in a little village called Shea. The Castle was huge, and Tim laughed at my mock "Oh my." James pulled right up to the door and it opened before we could get out of the car. A tiny, pretty woman in her forties wearing a smart black dress and hair in a bun, stepped out and stood to the side. "Welcome home, my lord," she said. Tim stopped and introduced me to her. "Clara, this is a very good friend of mine and a special guest. Please prepare the suite next to mine and a seat for her to my right at dinner. May I present Ms. Susan Chadworth? Sue, Clara has been with me for donkey's years and she runs this house with an iron fist. My butler, Granville, is on holiday. We will muddle on without him for now."

"Oh, go on with you my lord; I will see that Sandra takes excellent care of you, Ms. Chadworth."

James deposited my luggage by the door and a look from Clara had a nearby footman hustle them up the stairs to my new suite.

"Would you care to freshen up Ms. Chadworth; or would you like a drink first? Tea will be served in the drawing room, my lord."

"I will go in to tea, thank you, Clara." I said.

We had our tea, and then Tim showed me around the castle. We ended up on a balcony outside my window and he left me to get ready for dinner. He said they dressed for dinner but if I wasn't prepared, no one would care. I assured him I was prepared.

Sandra tapped on the door and said, "I have hung your frocks up and shaken them out miss. Would you like me to help you dress?" At a glance, I noted that Sandra was also in her forties and very pretty. I thanked her, but declined her assistance and went about choosing a suitable dress.

When I descended the huge stairway, Tim awaited me at the bottom, beautifully turned out, to take me in to dinner. I took his arm and we entered a huge dining hall. The table was elegant and set with the finest silver and china. Snowy white napkins were placed at each setting. The room had two other people seated at the table and Tim seated me to his right at the head of the table. The older woman seated to the left of Tim glowered at me and Tim introduced her as his Aunt Prudence. She grumped a barely civil acknowledgement and I was then presented to the gentleman to my right. "This is my cousin, Nigel Warren, Sue." Nigel rose and bent over my hand and said "Delighted." His hand was damp and clammy and I suppressed a shudder when he touched me. Tim's introduction of me as his very special guest had left conversation strained with his relatives, but he blithely chatted on to me about the estate, posing questions every now and then to his relatives. Instead of leaving me with his aunt after dinner, Tim took my hand and we all went into the parlor. It was a sumptuous room with silk wallpaper and a huge fireplace. We sipped coffee and made light conversation until Aunt Prudence excused herself for the evening and Nigel wasn't far behind her. Tim explained that though he called Prudence Warren "aunt" as she had married a second cousin to his father and Nigel was her son and next in line to his title as Tim was an only child and had no other living relatives. Nigel's father, Cliff Warren had died many years ago.

"How do you like your new home?" Tim asked. I looked at him and he grinned widely. "Surely you know there will never be another woman in my life Sue. From this moment on you are The Marchioness of Tottersham to me and I shall make that very legal as soon as I can." His highhanded statement thrilled me instead of angering me and I was more than ready to be his wife after one afternoon and evening. It was right and there was no other explanation. We retired to his master suite and our "wedding night," was the stuff dreams are made of.

Within the week we were married. The ceremony was actually quite crowded with various lords and ladies of the realm. A disapproving Prudence and Nigel attended as well. With the formal obligations taken care of and Tim's solicitor handling the necessary legal documents, I was presented to all on July 10ᵗʰ as The Marchioness of Tottersham. We then went on a long honeymoon to a little cottage that Tim owned in Kent. We whiled the long happy days away and pretended we didn't have to go back to all the pomp of the castle. Our time was precious and short-lived.

We returned to the castle in early September and Tim was dead within the week. He had fallen from a parapet while inspecting the castle roof. I determined to never go on a roof again. My darling was dead. I was in a state of shock. The inquest called it an accident and the wheels of the realm turned. After some kind of haggle among the solicitors, the new Lord Tottersham, Nigel, took over the title as the next legitimate heir in line and I was politely told to remove myself to the dowager house, which was my right as a widow and "titled" lady. I was given all my due very properly and was represented by Tim's solicitor. Lord Nigel informed me to be very careful as the estate could be very dangerous.

As my beloved Tim was gone, I closed up the property that was righted to me, left it in the hands of the solicitor, and along with my title and significant funds that I didn't need, I shook the dust of the castle and Shea from my feet and returned to the United States to mourn my short bout with total happiness. Sir Giles met an untimely death in Peter Trapton's last adventure book and I never wrote of him again.

I put the manuscript back in the envelope and shuddered. How horrible for my mother and father. They had done nothing but love each other and were rewarded with treachery. I determined to get to the bottom of the whole thing. I would have to tread with caution.

Chapter 13

I heard Clark arrive the next morning as I was finishing dressing. I had brought casual outfits and I slipped into a frilly light blue tee-shirt and white shorts that showed off my slim tanned thighs. I slipped my feet into some slip-on deck shoes and went down to the kitchen where Mary was bustling about with the brunch preparations. Clark was sitting at the table with a cup of coffee and chatting with her in a friendly way. Today, he wasn't Lieutenant Sanderson—he was just a very good friend of mine. When I came into the room he stood up and kissed me on the mouth. I saw Mary raise her eyebrows, but she went about her business. She served us a beautiful brunch. Clark thanked her politely and took my hand to lead me outside. I had asked Mary earlier if she would pack us a picnic lunch and she had a large basket complete with a fluffy blanket. I told her we were going across to Ellie's Island. She handed the basket to Clark and the blanket to me.

"Perry is at the boathouse waiting for you. He didn't know which boat you would want to take. They are always ready for you no matter which you want."

"Thanks, for everything, Mary. Expect us when you see us. We are taking the day off." We went down to the boathouse, talking on the way.

"I suppose you know how to jockey a boat in the bay as you come from around here. Which one do you want to use? I can usually hold my own with all of them if you can't."

Clark looked at the beautiful boats and decided to take the cruiser. "We can use the dinghy to get ashore on Ellie, if the dock isn't out this early."

Perry backed the large cabin cruiser out of the deep water boathouse and we went to the end of the dock to go aboard. After stowing our gear, we waved to Perry who stood on the dock with an unhappy look on his face. He wanted to go I expect.

We laughed as the wind blew our hair and the sun warmed our skin. It was a beautiful day. It took about fifteen minutes to get to Ellie's Island and we really enjoyed the boat ride. The dock was already out for the season and I jumped out to secure the boat to the dock. Clark passed the gear over the side to me and then jumped out as well. We turned and mutually carried everything up to the freshwater pond that was near a small copse of trees. Few people knew about this beautiful spot in Rigby Cove.

I spread the blanket and Clark dropped our gear near it. I went to the water's edge and reached up and pulled the combs from my hair, putting them in my shorts pocket. My hair fell halfway down my back and the breeze picked it up as I looked back at Clark. He was watching me with a hot look in his eyes. I lifted my shirt over my head. I didn't have on a bra and I removed my shorts. I was naked and he wasted no time in joining me. He was beautiful. My breath was coming in short bursts as he walked up to me and bent down to kiss me hard on the mouth. The blanket welcomed our aroused bodies and we made fast and furious love. The second time was slow and sweet. We were complete. We dozed in the sun and woke up together in each other's arms. We spent the afternoon eating and making slow beautiful love. Clark asked me to marry him and I was surprised at how fast I said yes. We began to talk.

"How well do you know Perry Dawson?" he asked. I looked at him in alarm and he said, "I know; you don't want to think he might be dangerous but we have to look at all of the people involved in your mother's life. How long have Perry and Mary worked at Rigby House?"

I tried to remember. "They have always been here since I can remember. Maybe the manuscripts will tell us. I have finished the first one and I think you should read them as well. I have a key to the library and can open the safe so we can get the others any time we want. I hid them there for protection until I could read them. We can go to my house in Trafton if you'd like to read them."

"I don't know how much reading we will accomplish." He smiled. "I was afraid once we put our hands on each other, there would be no peace."

"Worse things could happen," I laughed.

"That's what I am afraid of. I need to know you are safe, Thea, and I will spend every minute I can with you, until we have this case solved. Now my darling if you don't put your clothes on, we will still be here tomorrow."

We arrived back at Rigby House tired and happy. We carried the gear up from the boat and left it in the kitchen. Mary greeted us with a smile and asked if we would be in for supper.

"We are going in to Trafton and might not be back tonight. We have things to do." We went to the study and got the manuscript and then went to my room on the second floor. I stripped out of my clothes to take a shower and Clark groaned. Sand and half of Ellie's Island, was soon in my bed and we were very late getting to the library. I thought of mother's beautiful short time with my father and sincerely hoped Clark and I would be able to enjoy this happiness for a long, long time.

We pulled into the library parking lot just as Emmy was locking up. She waved and stopped what she was doing. We got out of Clark's car and went over to her.

"I guess you need more reading material," she said. "I am so glad I caught you. I need to tell you something. Carry has been checking out books on how to contest a will and she looks like she means business. She made a crack that my friend "her highness" wouldn't be so high in a little while. I am afraid that your family isn't taking your inheritance so well."

"Thanks for telling me, Emmy. I knew they were angry and I am sorry, but my mother knew what she was doing. The will is incontestable as they will find out. Mr. Severied told me he researched it for weeks, British laws included. My father's title was written in such a way that when a legitimate direct line, male or female, was not available, the nearest legitimate relative would inherit the title as Marquis or Marchioness. In the event no relation could be found, the title would expire. I am afraid the present Marquis of Tottersham is not the legal holder of the title. He didn't know my father had an heir and I understand he has no legal progeny either. That is why my mother was so afraid to keep me openly. You can let it be known now that she was really my mother, as I am not hiding it any longer. As for Hal and his family, there is a clause that they mustn't contest or they will forfeit their written inheritance. I am sure my mother thought long and hard to protect me, and I am confident that she succeeded. I will ask Mr. Severied to speak with Hal and alert him to the risk he is taking with his share. I don't wish them any ill will and in fact will make them known in my own will, but I have enough risk at the present to let that be known."

We opened the safe and took out the next copy of Mother's manuscripts. After securing the safe we locked and left the library. I lagged behind with Emmy for a minute and said, "By the way Em, Clark and I got engaged today. Are you shocked? We have known each other less than a week, but we are so happy."

Emmy squealed and hugged me hard, "No my sweet friend, I am so glad. When Bruce told me what Clark had told Hillary I wished that what he was telling her was for real. Bruce was standing right behind Hillary when Clark said you were his fiancée and he actually felt sorry for Hillary."

"I know, I felt sorry for her too, until she ruined my gloves and wrap."

"Be careful of her, Thea, she is dangerous and spoiled, and she wants Clark." She ran to Clark and hugged him too.

"I take it you have told our friend that we are going to get married," he said with a smile.

"I am so excited. Can I tell everyone? When is the wedding? Am I your bridesmaid?"

"Well, Em, we'd kind of like to tell everyone ourselves. We haven't given the wedding any thought yet, and of course you will be my bridesmaid. You can, however, tell everyone that Sue was my real mother. That should help you curb your excitement to tell all. We will probably be at my house in town for the next couple of days. Clark is going to be reading the manuscripts as well. We need information before we can continue with the investigation."

She hugged us again and went on her happy way. I was so fortunate to have her for my friend. She had never looked down on me because she was rich and I was an unknown. She was just a true friend.

Chapter 14

We stopped at a pizza place and drove over to my little house and ate at my kitchen table. Clark began to tell me all about his transformation from rich playboy to a local sheriff's department.

His great-great-grandfather, Louis Trafton, had settled the town and owned a large fishing fleet and operated a huge ship building firm. Granger was an ex-senator and a present district court judge and Clark had every advantage there was. He graduated law school with distinction and was fully prepared to follow in his father's footsteps. In his last year of law school a friend was accused of rape and murder and a small town deputy had worked like a dog and cleverly found the evidence to exonerate him. It was a life-changing experience for Clark. He saw the difference the deputy made in his friend's life and he wanted to feel that same sense of satisfaction. He came back to Trafton and joined the sheriff's department and by hard work, and not his father's position, he climbed his way up to lieutenant in very short order. At thirty one he had accomplished his goal. He was at peace, and now that he had Thea he was a completely happy man. He had to keep her safe. She had exploded into his universe and he would never be the same again.

"I have been working on the alibis for the time Susan was killed," he said. "I have worked through the list you gave me and have eliminated quite a few. There are some that I can't locate right now, but I will keep at it. We have to work it from all angles, Thea, and that includes Perry and Mary. I can detect a slight accent with Perry that doesn't quite fit down east, quite possibly British. I am checking on his citizenship. Mary seems like she has been around here for a long while. My mother remembers the Ameses have been here forever. So I think we can eliminate Mary."

"I am so glad. She has been so good to me my whole life, so has Perry. He taught me to fish and so many other things. I can't believe he would hurt Sue."

"Someone did—that is for sure. We know that she wouldn't have been safe in Britain, but she has lived here for twenty-five years without incident. There may or may not be a connection. I will write to a law school classmate of mine who lives in London now. I will ask him to check on each person that was at the castle when your father died. It was a long time ago so we must rely heavily on your mother's manuscript to help him out. We may have to eventually go to the castle ourselves and see what we can stir up."

"Oh Clark, you are giving me hope for the first time that we might actually get to the bottom of this. My mother was so forlorn after my father's death, she may have missed something. I believe if she was going to commit suicide, she would have done it then. Their love was so intense she was lost. I know how she felt—I can't believe how much you mean to me after such a short time. I want us to be able to move on with a clear conscience. I think we can do this. As far as my title and inheritance are concerned, I think you know that it is secondary to anything else in my life. If we have children, of course I want them to inherit their British heritage and titles if they want them. My father would want his grandson to assume the title and keep it alive. I have directed Mr. Severied to contact my father's solicitor and inform him that there is an heir apparent and to forward the proof of my birth. If we went to the castle, I am sure there would be fireworks. Nigel will have to vacate the castle and all of its properties as quickly as he made my mother leave. The estate manager and solicitor will be in charge until such a time when we can tend to it ourselves. If we are going to Britain, I would like to be married first. I need that protection for any heirs we might produce."

"Speaking of which, I think it is time to tell Mother and Dad that we are going to be married right away. I hope you don't have your heart set on a society wedding, because they take time. Mother and Arabella would pull out all stops and we would never get away. If they insist, we can have one later. I would like Dad to marry us in his chamber as quickly as possible to protect your reputation. I know people don't care as much about that now, but considering your position, I think we should care, for our children's sake."

"I am glad you understand all the ramifications facing us. It is not too late to back out you know. I will understand."

"Let's call Emmy and Bruce, and see if they can stand up with us as witnesses on Wednesday afternoon. That is my next day off and I am going to see the sheriff and arrange for a leave of absence. Now, let's go see my mother and dad."

We wasted no time in arriving at Clark's parent's home. It was a lovely old brick mansion set on gated grounds overlooking the bay in Trafton. We were greeted with enthusiasm by his parents and when they heard our plans they asked no questions, and we made the arrangements for Wednesday. We told them about Sue being my mother and all the details of the investigation. Granger was very interested and quickly told us that if he could help in any way to let us know. Sylvia hugged us both and said she would do what she could to make it a pretty wedding. We left them happily making plans and Clark wanted me to see his house. He turned down a little side street by the bay and stopped in front of a house that looked so much like mine that I laughed. He said, "I thought you might like it. Our tastes are so much alike right down to the front porch rockers."

We went inside and it was indeed very much like mine. His décor was more masculine, but the rest was very similar. He explained that he too needed a place to call his own and that this small house had fit the bill. We checked everything out and decided to stay the night there. We had brought our manuscripts, and settled down to read in his pleasant little study in front of an open fire. Clark picked up manuscript number one and I took number two and sat in a matching chair to his. We read:

Rigby House welcomed me home. I had not really lived in the house, but had loved it at first sight. I had purchased it when my writing career had first taken off and I decided I would need some help to keep it in good order. I quickly advertised for a jack of all trades and a cook housekeeper. I just wanted to go to ground and keep my nose to the grindstone and try to forget.

61

Two weeks after I placed the ad, the doorbell rang. It was a plump little woman who introduced herself as Mary Ames. She was about thirty and said she had just lost her husband at sea. She had no children and had no problem with living in. I showed her the little suite beside the kitchen and she said it was so cute she could cry. I guessed Mary was in pretty dire straits and we wasted no time getting her settled. My lawyer Henry Severied vouched for her as a local woman fallen on hard times. He said she had been away for a few years. I told her to decorate the suite to her taste and she settled in the next day.

I had hired a firm to take care of the yard work while I was away so I didn't fret when no one answered my ad for a handy man right away. I did continue to advertise and several applicants came out to Rigby House, but I was particular and they didn't suit somehow.

I settled in to write, keeping my study locked and Mary understood that it was never to be entered and was totally private. If she wondered why I would lock myself up for days on end and sometimes come out red eyed from crying, she didn't comment. She was the perfect companion. She kept to her job and I kept to mine.

I seemed to have picked up a bug as I was quite unwell. After several weeks of no appetite and feeling nauseous, I woke up one morning quite ill and had an epiphany. I was pregnant! Oh, how wonderful! I had a part of Tim right with me forever. I jumped for joy. I needed to tell the world!

Wait, I couldn't let anyone know. My baby was in danger. I needed to think. I made an appointment with a good obstetrician in Portland and confirmed my diagnosis. I then called my old friend and lawyer Henry Severied and made an appointment for after hours in his office in Rigby.

Henry was glad to see me and listened to my story with troubled eyes. He agreed that to be sure my child was never harmed I could not acknowledge it for now. I grieved so hard he devised a plan. When I was six months pregnant and hardly showing at all, I told Mary I was going on a research trip and went away to Portland and rented a house. Henry would visit me each week and fill me in on what he was doing about my affairs both here and in London. When I went into labor on May 21ˢᵗ I called Henry and he came to be with me. My daughter was born that same day. I stayed in my rented house for two days with my precious daughter. I knew even then she was going to be the best child in the world and I could not even see her. I had a brother who lived in Portland

and Henry took her to my brother's wife, Wanda, rang the bell and waited behind a shrub for her to come to the door. He said she was flabbergasted until she read the note.

We had written: My name is Thea. Please contact Mr. Henry Severied and he will establish that you will be paid to raise me as your own. My parents cannot keep me, but you will be paid fifty thousand dollars a year to stand in. Mr. Severied will also see that any needs that I might have will be promptly paid for. Please read the enclosed contract and by accepting and cashing the enclosed cashier's check for fifty thousand dollars, I have become your "niece." Please call Mr. Severied for an appointment and he will see that your contract is honored in full. The other check for twenty thousand is to be used to see that I am properly set up in a nursery and properly attired. Please call Mr. Severied with any question, the number is attached.

Wanda wasted no time in calling Henry and he assured her the baby was of good heritage, but due to circumstances beyond the parents' control they could not keep her. He told her that she would receive the fifty thousand dollars every year until Thea was educated and able to fend for herself, at which time the contract would expire, and all obligations on her part would cease. He told her that an additional forty thousand dollars would be provided each year for clothing and other needs. If more was needed for any reason, they were to contact him. Her every need was to be taken care of.

My brother's wife is a social climber, but otherwise a kind woman in her own way. I just hoped she would be kind to my sweet Thea. She saw the chance to get lots of money very easily and as I was hoping, she grabbed at it. The contract stated she needed to raise Thea with the name Thea Chadworth so she would not be embarrassed as an orphan. Henry provided proper documents to that effect.

I came home to Rigby House and Mary welcomed me. She said a man had applied for the handy man position and she had asked him to leave a number. She said he seemed well spoken and knew all about boats, cars, and landscaping. He had left a number and I called him. When he answered the phone he seemed to have a British accent, but as he talked to me it seemed to be more down east. I asked him to come for a face-to-face meeting and I liked what I saw. I hired Perry Dawson and he completed our threesome that lives in Rigby House. We rub along nicely together, not bothering each other and he too understands that is how I am.

A few weeks after I returned home, my brother Hal and his wife and family came for a rare visit. They had their own boy and girl and my own beautiful daughter. I had to act surprised as they told me the story of their good fortune. They had moved to a nice house in Trafton and Hal had purchased a hardware store. They were very happy. Wanda was very good with the baby and tried to make sure nothing ever happened to her. I was dying to hold Thea, but as I was not overly fond of Carry and Tony, I could not fuss over Thea. I should be grateful for small things. My beautiful daughter had come home.

The tears streaming down my face alerted Clark to my sorrow. I had finished my manuscript and could not believe what my mother had gone through to keep me safe. He had finished his as well and we soon retired for the night.

Chapter 15

Time went by so quickly that before we could turn around it was Tuesday night. I had had a busy couple of days and Emmy was a huge help. We shopped for dresses and got our hair done as well as all the other things we had to do. Word had gotten out (by Emmy of course) and it seemed as if the whole town congratulated Clark and me. I invited the Chadworths and Wanda declined without asking Hal. It made me sad; they had raised me—even if they did it for the money. Uncle Hal called me later that day and said he was sorry that Wanda and the kids had acted that way. He said that Carry had been hanging out with Hillary Leighton for the last couple days and he was worried they might do something. He said Carry had told him that Hillary hated me with all her being and of course Carry is flattered that Hillary wants to be her friend. He said he wished he had known I was his real niece before because he had to keep himself from loving me and was afraid I would be taken away. He said he wound up loving me anyway as I was such a sweet little girl. He warned me to be careful and not take the girls for granted. He would keep an eye on Carry as he felt she was headed for trouble with Hillary. I told him we were going to England for a while so not to worry for now. I gave him my cell number and wished him well and told him I loved him too.

We stayed at Rigby House on Tuesday as we wanted Sue to be in on our wedding. Silly, I know, but Clark indulged me. He left early and I followed later with Perry and Mary arriving last at the Sandersons' mansion. They were pleased to be invited. Our small wedding was proving to be not so small as Sylvia had worked non-stop on all the plans. The house was filled with flowers and people. Emmy rushed me to the "bridal room" upstairs where my dress and accessories waited. The wedding march started as I reached the top of the stairway and when I reached the bottom behind Emmy, Granger met me and walked me down the make-shift aisle in the huge parlor. Clark waited near a floral arbor and Granger stopped and passed my hand to Clark. He was stunning. My dress was gorgeous, Emmy had seen to that and my veil was flowers entwined in my hair, but Clark outshone the bride in his white tuxedo and big grin.

Granger stepped forward and turned to the crowd and began the service. It was very moving and he had the people in tears.

"My dear friends and family, please know that Sylvia and I could not be happier with our only son's choice of a bride. She is the daughter we have always wanted and we hope they provide us with many grandchildren." The people laughed and I blushed. He went on to marry us in a ceremony fit for a cathedral. When he pronounced us man and wife and said Clark could kiss his bride his son wasted no time in doing just that.

Aunt Arabella and Uncle Frank greeted us with effusion and Clark introduced me to his cousin Andrew who was with them. Andrew bowed over my hand and said, "Clark always did have impeccable taste." He was very good looking in all the Sanderson's blond way and he was just as big a man as Clark. He punched Clark on the arm with a grin. We mingled for an hour and then made our excuses.

We left the small reception that was very posh for all its size and went straight to the library. We opened the safe and took out two more manuscripts. We planned on reading, as well as other "stuff" on our honeymoon.

We drove back to Clark's house on the water and sat on the porch for a while to just savor the fact we were man and wife. We held hands and drank some fine champagne that Arabella had given us. Clark mentioned that the final alibis for the rest of the people on my list of Susan's guests at Rigby House had been proven. We were at a standstill on that. He said that Perry had immigrated to America years ago and he was from Britain. We didn't know what to think of that except to wait and see.

Chapter 16

We went in after a while and sat in our chairs in front of the fireplace. Clark said he would make a call to his friend in London and I started to read manuscript number three. It was dated the year I was three years old. It read:

On Hal's last visit I showed a rare flash of hospitality and invited them all for Christmas. I had much fun preparing the house and buying gifts. I asked Hal to make it a tradition and he agreed. I got Thea and Carry dolls that were very pretty and Carry squealed over hers. Thea thanked me nicely, laid her doll in its bed and covered her with a dolly quilt, then went straight to the little packet of books that I had bought on a whim and reverently picked them up. Her green eyes shone with happiness and she breathed in and out with excitement; her mother's daughter, I would see that she had every book she wanted from that time on. I caught my own breath as I realized how much she looked like Tim. "Had I made a mistake? Was she in danger?"

When Thea was three I asked if the children would like to visit for a couple weeks in the summer. Carry and Tony promptly declined. They would miss their friends and activities. I held my breath as little Thea piped up that she would love to visit with Aunt Sue for the summer. Wanda was embarrassed and started to fuss, but I said that she would be no bother as Mary and Perry liked her and it would give Wanda a nice break. She agreed reluctantly and Thea's face was so happy, it broke my heart. I could hardly wait for summer. I shopped for new toys and books and put them in Thea's room. When Hal brought her over she jumped out of the car with her little bag and rushed up to me. "Auntie Sue, can we go out in the boat? I love the water!" Hal said, "Now Thea, your Aunt Sue doesn't have time for stuff like that. You be a good girl and don't be making a nuisance of yourself."

Perry stepped forward and said, "Well, Mr. Chadworth, I reckon I can find the time to take little Thea for a ride in the boat. She is very well behaved and we will rub along just fine." Thea beamed and said, "Thank you, thank you Uncle Perry, I'll be ever so good, just wait and see." Perry's face flushed with pleasure and he smiled.

Mary said, *"Now little one let's go see what we can find for a snack and then maybe there are some new books in your room."* Thea took Mary's hand and they left to go to the kitchen. I could hear her chatter. *"Thank you, Aunt Mary."*

Hal said, *"Are you sure you want to put up with a young one around here, Sue? She really is a pretty easy child to tolerate. I wish my own kids were as nicely behaved."*

"I assure you she will be fine, Hal. She can stay as long as she likes. She seems to like it here and she is no bother to me at all."

After Hal had gone, I went to my room and closed the door. I mustn't cry. Take what I could and if I was just another aunt to her, so be it.

I stood outside Thea's room and listened to her chat with Mary. I had changed her room to a larger one with a bath and told Mary it was because she was staying longer this time. It was just down the hall from my room and I thought I might be able to sneak in and watch her while she slept. Mary had put all of her books and toys into special cupboards that Perry had built for her and I could hear her jabbering with pleasure.

"See all the new books Aunt Sue got for me. I just love Aunt Sue." I turned around and left as quickly as I could and went into my study downstairs. I was as happy as I could be right now.

Chapter 17

I put the finished manuscript away as Clark came back into the room. He said his friend was compiling quite a dossier on everyone at Tottersham Castle and I couldn't wait to hear what he had to say. It seems there was quite a stir made when Tim was killed. The solicitors unearthed the fact that Tim's father, Lord Randall, had two illegitimate sons and that the oldest one fully expected to inherit the title and estate. When he was informed that as an illegitimate son he could not inherit, he disappeared and has never been heard from since. He had been sent to America, by Lord Randall Tottersham, to get an education and he became quite spoiled. The other son had stayed on at the castle choosing to get his education in Britain and working on the estate under Herschel Dennis, who had been with Lord Randall as estate manager for years. He frequently traveled to Lord Tottersham's other properties outside Britain to keep them running smoothly. He too had left the castle shortly after learning of Tim's death and made frequent visits at the estate and the outlying properties for Lord Nigel. All reports were that Lord Nigel was not much interested in the day to day running of the estate and was more than happy to allow Herschel and Lord Randall's youngest illegitimate son to do so, being perfectly secure in the knowledge that he was the rightful heir. Much to his mother's dismay, he had no interest in producing an heir of his own as he was very involved with the gay community and his mousy little wife, Eileen, had not conceived any progeny.

"Glen is still checking on some of the others. He will get back to us soon. I will read this next manuscript and then it's bed for me."

I went to take a long bath and think on the new information I had learned. I was so exhausted that Clark found me sound asleep when he came to bed. He left me sleeping the next morning as he left for work early. He had a lot to do.

I had just woken up and discovered my new husband was not in the house, when the phone rang. It was Clark. "I just got the results of Sue's autopsy! She was poisoned," he said. "It was nicotine poison—the kind they use for gardening. I am on my way out to Rigby House to check the sheds."

I sat down in a kitchen chair. I was stunned. I needed to go to Rigby House. I wanted to know what was going on.

I arrived shortly after Clark and he was talking to Perry. They were on their way to the garden sheds and Perry was very upset. I caught up with them just as they got to the large garden shed that housed all of Perry's supplies. He had lawn mowers and all kinds of garden tools as well as pesticide treatments for the many shrubs and flowers he tended. He took Clark right to the shelf that held his nicotine supply.

"It's too early in the year for me to use much of this stuff, but here it is. Wait a minute, this has been messed with. I always keep this special container it comes in way to the back of the shelf, just like the rat poison and other harsh chemicals that I use on the property. I got in the habit of keeping it on the highest shelf and way to the back when Thea was little, I didn't want her to accidently get into it. This container is not on the right shelf and it is not properly sealed. Lieutenant, I know it looks bad for me, but I swear I would never do anything to hurt Sue or Thea. Please believe me, I loved Sue and I couldn't love Thea more if she was my own child." There were tears in his eyes and I went to him and hugged him. "Uncle Perry, I love you too and I know you wouldn't hurt me or my mother."

"You haven't called me Uncle since you were about six when Mary told you we weren't really your aunt and uncle. She was trying to explain our relationship to you. I really missed you calling me that, little one. I tried to tell you I liked you to call me that but you said it wasn't proper. I did draw the line at you calling me Mr. Dawson, you little rascal."

Clark told him he was taking the nicotine in for a test, but there wasn't much doubt in our minds that the poison that killed my mother came from that container. Perry said that every building on the property was going to get new locks and be kept locked even when he was there. I went into the house and checked that the study was still locked and not disturbed. Everything seemed to be in order. All the stuff I had found in the closet cubby was still where I had put it. I said hello to Mary, checked the rest of the house and left for Trafton. Clark had gone on ahead.

I went to the library and took the remaining four manuscripts out of the safe. I wanted to read them as quickly as possible. I had a feeling I couldn't shake that a clue was hidden somewhere in them. I said goodbye to Emmy and went back to Clark's house to get the fourth manuscript. I wanted to read them in order. I then drove to my own little house and settled in for the afternoon. I ate a small lunch and went to my study and began to read.

Chapter 18

Thea is coming today, it is her sixth birthday. She is so beautiful. I am so afraid someone who knew Tim will see her. She is the spitting image of him. Her long curly auburn hair is the same exact shade as her father's. When Mary is not around I brush it for her and arrange it with pretty barrettes. She chatters away and I cherish these times with her. I wish she could stay with me forever, but I can't have her in fear for her life before she needs to. Sometimes, I feel that I should just forget her heritage and keep her with me, but then I think of how much Tim loved his estate and would want his child to have it and I can't risk anyone knowing about her yet.

He had talked about his childhood growing up at the castle. He hadn't known his mother. She died when he was two. The Marchioness Althea Hottersham had been sickly and after producing an heir she gave up trying. Lord Randall Hottersham had been a very virile man and built up quite a reputation with the ladies. He was however, as far as Tim was concerned, the world's greatest father. He spent time with him and his two friends at the castle. Colin Pierce was Sandra's son and three years younger than Tim. Clara's son, Granville, as Tim called him, was also younger than him by three and a half years and Granville was his favorite. He never did call him by his real name because he liked Granville after a character in a book they had both read. Granville played at being the butler at the castle and they all had a great time growing up together. Tim was never treated as the master of the house and they were all equal. His father had even sent the other two to great universities. Colin chose America and Granville and Tim went to the same school in Britain. When Randall was killed in Africa in an accident at one of his properties, Tim at the age of twenty-two was suddenly thrown into the running of the estate and Colin seemed to resent the fact that he was no longer an equal. Granville on the other hand took to the situation with relish and threw himself into the role of butler and factotum as a lark and did it when he pleased. They played hard but worked hard as well.

I wanted Thea and her children to enjoy the same things her father did, but Thea was missing out on all of it through no fault of her own. I would have to make her life as enjoyable as I could in order to save it.

The next manuscript continued in the same vain as she reminisced about my growing up and the fun we had had with Perry and the boats.

I continued to read through the afternoon manuscript after manuscript.

I have learned that Nigel has no children and that he is probably gay. His poor wife has a large cross to bear. My solicitor has informed me that my little dowager house and grounds are being well maintained by Herschel and Granville. I try to keep in touch any way that I can.

I have tried to counsel Thea in her choice of college and courses and she has chosen a nice liberal arts school with the best studies available. She has learned that I have funded a library and her goal is to become a librarian. I told her that if an opening is available when she is through with her schooling, she can apply but I would not interfere and she would have to make it on her own merits. She agreed that she wanted it that way or not at all.

Thea graduated from high school today and I am so proud of her. I hired a photographer to take pictures of her without her knowledge. I attended with Perry and we sat at the back of the room. The Chadworths didn't attend and Thea's eyes found us in the back and she beamed at us. Perry patted my hand.

She has gone away to college and I miss her dropping in to chat. Perry and I have been boating recently and find that relieves our loneliness for her.

My darling has graduated from college and again Perry and I made the trip to see her graduate. When we returned home we sat on the dock and I stared out at the water. Perry was very quiet.

He finally said, "Sue, I need to tell you something. I am Tim's and Colin's half brother. We grew up together knowing that and couldn't be closer. Colin didn't know until Tim was killed that he couldn't ever inherit because he was illegitimate and he was very angry. He was several months older than me and Lord Randall took more caution with his dalliances after me. My mother told me he regularly visited her and Sandra and in payment took excellent care of them and their sons. I know that Thea is Tim's daughter and you are her mother. I see the love and anguish on your face when you are with her. I know you fear for her life and I have tried to help protect her for as long as I have known. I have known since she was very small. She is the very image of Tim and I have tried to find out who is a threat to her at the castle. I suspected Nigel at first but decided he just didn't have the nerve. He is all talk. I even suspected his mother, my father's second cousin's wife, but she isn't strong enough to have pushed Tim off that parapet. It had to be someone that Tim trusted. I have concluded that it must have been Colin as he left shortly after Tim's death and no one has heard from him since." He looked at me and saw my white face. "Oh, Sue, I am so sorry. I have shocked you too much. I came here under false pretences to watch over you for Tim's sake in case Colin should take it in his head to hurt you. Tim called me and told me about you on your wedding day. He was so happy I knew he would finally settle down and have a family and heir. Someone else must have thought so too. They didn't want anyone else between them and the title. I can only think it was Colin."

I sat there stunned. What Perry had told me all added up. I had met Sandra's son but didn't remember meeting Perry.

"I don't remember meeting you, Perry," I said.

"Tim would have called me Granville." He smiled. "Our own little joke, he never called me anything else. I was away on one of my jaunts. No one but Tim knew where I was. By the time I came home he was entombed in the castle crypt and you were long gone. I fell into deep grief for Tim. I knew I had to find you and watch out for you. It took me a while to realize Tim's solicitor would know how to find you and now I won't leave until you tell me to."

"I don't want you to leave," I said. "We have to think how to protect Thea and see that she gets her rightful place."

Thea applied to the library in Trafton. When the board considered her application I made no mention of my interest in her, but the others accepted her with alacrity. They felt lucky to have her and indeed we were. She is making many wonderful changes.

Perry and I have decided to tell Thea the truth. Perry is going back to the castle next week to check the lay of the land so to speak. He has gone back to check on the estate and Herschel keeps things together when he is not there. It is time for one of his visits.

I will put this last manuscript in the bank safety deposit box. Mary knows nothing of any of this and Perry has not told her of our closeness.

Chapter 19

I had to find Clark and let him know that Perry is telling the truth.

The phone rang and it was Clark. I began to babble at him.

"Hey, slow down," he said. "I called to let you know Sue's body is released and you can tend to the arrangements if you want. I know that she didn't want anyone there, but I think she would understand your need to be there. They are burying her this evening in her private lot."

"We need to call Perry and let him know. I will explain what I have found out when you get home. I need to talk with Perry right now!"

I called Rigby House and Mary answered. I asked to speak with Perry and she said he had gone to town. I thanked her and wished her well. I called Mr. Severied and asked him a question. He said he would help me and make the arrangements I wanted. It was now one o'clock and I had a million things to do.

I grabbed a yellow pad and began scribbling furiously.

The doorbell rang. I went to the door and Perry stood there. He looked tired and apprehensive. I pulled him in and closed the door.

"I need to talk to you, Thea. I can't sleep and I am so worried."

"I know everything, Uncle Perry. I am so glad you are my real uncle. Mother left manuscripts and I have just finished them. She told how she felt about you and I know you wouldn't have hurt her. I need to ask you some questions and then we need to get busy. We need to go to the castle and we are taking Mother with us."

I got on the phone. I talked with Sylvia and explained everything that was going on. Clark had told me he was finishing up his last shift and headed my way. I called Mr. Severied again and he had already made great strides in our plans. We had less than ten hours to accomplish all we had to do. We had to be at the airport in Bangor around midnight and it was a two-hour drive to get there.

Perry stood by, wringing his hands while I whirled like a dervish. I called Emmy and asked her to come help me. She said she would leave Temple in charge and be here shortly. I took a little leather attaché case and assembled all the things I would need for paperwork. Mr. Severied would handle the rest. Thank God I had a current passport and visa. Mother had seen to that. I had traveled with Emmy abroad on funds provided by Mr. Severied when I was in school. Perry was slowly gathering what I was up to and got into the swing of things quickly. He too began to make notes.

Clark came through the door only to be hit by a tornado and after a quick update, he sprung into action. He left for his house to get his passport and luggage. As a senator's son, he was well versed in what he would need to function at the castle.

Perry and I tore out of town to Rigby House and met a distracted Mary at the door. I explained that Clark and I were going on an extended honeymoon and Perry was leaving early on his trip and driving us to the airport. She muttered her way back to the kitchen and I flew into my mother's study after using my locket key to open the door. The key stuck a little but worked on the second try. I rushed to the box with my mother's papers and picked up the framed picture of my father. I took a framed publicity photo of my mother off the wall and rushed back out the door. I took the time to lock it again and met Perry in the drive. He had his bags with him as he had been prepared to leave next week anyway.

Perry drove back into Rigby and we stopped at the funeral home where they had taken Mother to be prepared. Mr. Severied had already made the arrangements and they were expecting me. I asked them to put the framed photos in the coffin and made sure the hearse and driver would be ready for the motorcade to the airport. Perry and I then chose a beautiful cream-colored casket worthy of a marchioness and we drove back to my house in Trafton. Emmy had arrived and had taken charge. She had my luggage all ready with plenty of dress gowns and proper business suits. She had also taken the manuscripts back to the safe at the library. I was so grateful she had thought of everything.

Perry was putting my luggage in the large estate SUV he had been driving, just as Clark arrived with his needed luggage. We decided to take Clark's Mercedes, too. I noticed Emmy's car was packed to the windows. She saw me looking and grinned. "You didn't think you could get away without me did you? Bruce will be here shortly. He is going too."

Clark laughed and said, "Some honeymoon." He took my hand and said, "I hope you don't mind Thea, but when I stopped by Mother's house, she had the town car loaded down with luggage and Aunt Arabella and Uncle Frank were just pulling in with their luggage in their town car as well. Dad said we would need all of our legal expertise and there was also safety in numbers."

I laughed. "We should be plenty safe then. I hope Mr. Severied hired a big enough plane."

Clark said, "Uncle Frank called Mr. Severied and we are taking the Vermillion jet to London. It is fueled and waiting for us at the Bangor International Airport.

Chapter 20

We all met up with Mr. Severied at the funeral home in Rigby, and with the hearse leading the procession we headed for Bangor in our motorcade. Mother hadn't wanted any fanfare for her funeral, but she couldn't have imagined what a difference it would make for her to be murdered as a still young woman and she was going back to Tim in the pomp and circumstance she deserved.

We arrived at the airport with time to spare and the coffin was reverently loaded in the cargo space with our luggage. The plane was packed. We put all of our various vehicles in long-term parking and boarded the plane. We made quite a crew.

Uncle Frank's jet had all the comforts of home. There were two well-rested pilots and two stewards to serve us and as none of us had taken the time to eat a meal, we were all starving. We were served a delicious meal in a surprisingly large dining area and after talking about our plans, with Henry Severied (Did I tell you he had come with us?) filling us in on what waited for us in London, we all lowered our luxury seats and tried to sleep. Only Mr. Severied, Clark, Emmy, and Perry knew it was my twenty-fifth birthday.

Perry had phoned his mother to let her know that we were coming and to prepare enough rooms for all of us. She told him that the powers that be had informed Nigel that he was being replaced as heir to the title and the proof would be with us. She said Prudence was furious and they were all in a tizzy. He told her he would call her back to let her know the exact time of our arrival.

We arrived in London at one o'clock London time and were met by all the officials that needed to carry out the transfer of title. We were also met by a first class funeral home director with a stately hearse waiting for the transfer of mother's coffin. Arabella and Sylvia had been on the phone all morning and everything was in place. Mr. Severied was greeted by the officials that would travel with us to Tottersham Castle and he rode with them. He had with him all the papers necessary to prove that I was heir to the title.

We again had a number of limousines waiting and our luggage was quickly loaded in a transport vehicle as well. We were all very tired and excited.

Mr. Severied, Granger, and Uncle Frank along with the two officials of the realm were in a stretch limo with a table for their business discussions and the rest of us traveled in another limo that left us plenty of room to talk and maneuver. This vehicle was directly behind the hearse and again we made a lengthy procession as we headed out of London for Tottersham Castle. Perry called his mother and told her we were about an hour out and would be there shortly.

Perry had made arrangements for a vicar to be there to enter Mother with honor in a small ceremony at the family crypt. That would be first on our agenda after I had talked with Nigel.

We swept up the drive to the castle and to my amazement every inhabitant of the castle was standing on the wide circular steps. The servants were to the left and Nigel and Prudence to the right facing the steps.

We exited the vehicles and Perry acting as the formal butler of Tottersham Castle stated in a loud voice as he pulled me forward "The Marchioness Timothea Claire Chadworth Tottersham."

I stepped forward to applause from the castle inhabitants and smiled at them.

"It is good to be home," I said.

Nigel stepped forward and took my hand. Mother was right, it was cold and clammy; he spoke in a quiet voice. "I hope you will consider that I have held the title with honor and have been a good steward for the estate, when you make plans for my mother, Eileen and me."

I withdrew my hand and refrained from wiping it on my skirt. "I will give you the same consideration you gave my mother when she was a grief stricken young widow. You and your family may retire to the dowager house for now, until I make my final decision. Please see that you remove yourself from the castle today. We are going to the family crypt for a short ceremony to place my mother next to my father in the crypt. You are all welcome to attend." I raised my voice to include everyone on the steps. Nigel recoiled with a look of surprise and his mother burst into tears. I ignored them. I turned to the servant side of the steps and smiled at the people assembled there. Perry stepped forward and began to introduce them to me one at a time. He began with his mother Clara. She was a tiny dark-haired woman of about sixty dressed in a very stylish black dress. I took her hand and said, "Thank you for being so kind to my mother while she was at the castle—she wrote of your kindness to her."

"I was very glad to have her with us even for such a short time. Please accept my belated condolences for the loss of both of your parents. Perry has told me a lot about you. I feel I know you very well."

We moved on to footmen, James the chauffer, cooks, maids and various other workers of the castle. We came to Sandra Pierce and I held out my hand. She took it with a limp handshake.

"My mother spoke of you as well, Mrs. Pierce. Thank you for your help to her." Sandra Pierce looked at me as if she was trying to tell whether I was being sarcastic or not; she looked away as soon as I released her hand. "I was looking forward to meeting your son as well, but I am told you haven't heard from him in a while. I hope you hear from him soon." She turned and rushed into the castle and I said to Clara, "I am sorry, did I say the wrong thing?"

"No, dear," Clara said. "She is very sensitive about Colin but you couldn't have known that. I have prepared a meal for after the service and your rooms are all ready." She indicated the rest of my party still standing on the steps.

"Oh dear, shall I take care of that now?"

"No, Mrs. Dawson. We are going directly to the crypt for the service and then we will retire to our rooms to freshen up for dinner. Will you see that the master suite is thoroughly cleaned and prepared for my husband and me?"

"Please call me Clara, and I will certainly see to it right now my Lady."

"Clara it is then and please, everyone, you must call me Thea."

The vicar stepped forward and introduced himself, then Clark took my arm, and we all followed the vicar to the crypt that was located to a side entrance to the castle. It was under a small chapel and the vicar intoned a brief interment ceremony and then the funeral attendants moved Mother to the place next to my father. Everyone but Clark left me and I spent a few moments of reverence with my mother and my father. Clara had already shown everyone to their suites and our luggage had been dispatched to the correct rooms. Mr. Severied had paid and tipped the funeral director and sent them on their way. Perry was already dressed in a very smart outfit that pegged him as the butler. I grinned. "Up to your old tricks again, Granville?" He grinned back, and bowed Clark and me into the master suite.

Clark, being used to such opulence, didn't stand with his mouth open as I did. He laughed at my look of astonishment and said, "What did you expect, Thea? You are a marchioness after all."

I laughed and slowly took in the suite. It was sumptuous and I wondered if my mother had been as awed as I was. From the velvet drapes to the silk wallpaper and thick carpets and stately bedroom furniture it was magnificent. I wished I could have discussed all this with her.

There was a rumble at the door and Emmy burst in with a shriek, "Really, Thea, do you believe all this? What a blast!"

"Come in Em," I said. "Don't stand on ceremony."

She laughed. "Sorry, I forget you are royalty and need your privacy." She grinned.

"Let us change and then we can all go down to dinner and face the music."

The officials of the realm had already shown Nigel the proof of Tim's paternity and he could not dispute the claim. He calmly removed himself from the castle along with his wife Eileen and a very disgruntled Prudence. Prudence was upset that they couldn't even stay for dinner, but I told her that it was a private party. We had invited the officials to stay for the meal, but they had to return to London so it was just the nine of us as Perry wanted to eat with his mother.

We ignored protocol for this one time and we dispersed ourselves around the table as we chose, eating and moving to another spot for conversation as the spirit moved us. We just plain needed to relax and have fun. After a while Perry came in and sat with us and joined in the revelry.

Finally, we fell into our beds exhausted.

Chapter 21

The next morning a tap on the door was followed by Sandra entering the room to inquire if we wanted breakfast in bed. She was still sullen and looked like she hadn't slept much. I wondered if she thought her son was responsible for all my trouble.

"No, we will come down to the dining room. We will be there in half an hour. Please tell the others that they may either dine in their rooms or eat with us."

"Very good, my Lady," Sandra said. She bowed out of the door.

"I don't think I care for someone tapping and entering our room. I think I will have to address some of the ways of the castle," I said to Clark. He was just waking up and his curly blond hair was mussed and he was beautiful. "Good morning, my handsome husband," I said. He pulled me down for a kiss and we were delayed a little getting to the dining room.

We met Perry at the bottom of the staircase and he said he would be available after breakfast for a tour of the castle and grounds if we were up to it.

"Oh Perry, that is exactly what I want to do this morning. We have so much to do and we need your help." He bowed us into the room ahead of him. Everyone else was already there and Clara had set the table with care, hoping, I suppose that we would adhere to protocol today and sit where we were supposed to. I relaxed the rules enough to seat Clark at the head of the table and Granger on the other end. I sat at Clark's right and Sylvia to his left. Frank sat next to Sylvia and Arabella sat to his left. Bruce sat to my right and Emmy sat to his right. Mr. Severied was to Emmy's right. The table had been reduced to the point that it was easy to converse. We chatted amiably while breakfast was served. Perry told us that usually the food was laid out on the sideboard and each person helped themselves, but Clara wanted everyone to feel at ease and the cook had joined in the idea to serve a sit down meal for breakfast. The meal was a delight and we all enjoyed ourselves.

"Perry, please give our compliments to Mrs. Henderson. Her cooking is divine."

"She will be pleased, Thea. No one has much appreciated her lately. You will find that most of the employees here have been here for years and years."

"We will have to see that they are appreciated more then. Where do you want us to meet you, Perry?"

"I think we should start inside and continue outside. Everyone is welcome to accompany us on the tour if you like," Perry said.

No one else was inclined to traipse around the castle all day so it was just Clark, Perry, and me. He showed us all around, from the top to the bottom wine cellar. It certainly was impressive and my mind boggled that I was responsible for all of this and the people that ran it. The castle was resplendent and Clark and I had great fun with my Uncle Perry, getting to know our way around. When we exited to the outside, Perry began to talk quietly. "Thea, you must be careful; Colin knows this castle like the back of his hand and if he intends to hurt you out of spite—and I can only conclude that is why Sue was murdered—he will be trying to do you harm."

Clark moved to my side and put his arm around me. He said, "Perry, we will all have to keep our eyes and ears open. I hope you know how much I appreciate you watching over Sue and Thea all these years, but we can't let our guard down—especially now."

We were standing in the garden on a stone walkway right under where my father had fallen to his death and I looked up at the roof of the castle. I shrieked, "Look out!" and pushed Clark and Perry out of the way just as a giant gargoyle crashed on the walkway beside us, strewing rocks around. We were stunned and hit by some of the rocks but we weren't hurt badly. Some debris had left bruises on us in various places. Clark and Perry tore into the castle and up the stairs to the roof. I went to find Clara and she put ointment on my cuts and bruises.

"Who could have done such a thing?" Clara said. "I didn't think Mr. Colin was here. I can't imagine anyone else trying to harm you, my lady."

"We must all be alert to danger until Clark puts an end to this nightmare."

Perry and Clark came looking for me and Clara addressed their wounds also. They said there was nobody on the roof by the time they had arrived there and the gargoyle was one of two that was placed on the stone parapet. They are very heavy and it would take great strength to move one.

"Do you think Nigel would do this, Perry?" Clark asked.

"I don't know. Whoever did this is not wasting time in trying to kill Thea. Let's go talk with Nigel and see where he was when it happened."

We found the others in our party gathered in the study just relaxing. They were appalled when they heard what had happened in the garden.

"Thea, do you think it wise to stay here?" asked Sylvia.

"I can't let them drive me away now. We are getting too close. I must find out who killed my mother and father and tried to kill us just now."

Clark said, "We are going down to the dowager house to talk with Nigel and Prudence. I am sure they will alibi each other but maybe one of the employees saw something. We will gather them for questioning when we return."

Chapter 22

Nigel, Eileen and Prudence were having a leisurely lounge in the garden of the dowager house when the three of us arrived. Nigel was as belligerent as he dared to, knowing that he was at my mercy to stay here. Prudence was outright furious.

"What makes you think you are so precious that we would bother with you? You have thrown us out of our home after Nigel kept the estate for you all these years. You should be grateful instead of resentful. Some people have no breeding."

Perry spoke up angrily. "Prudence, make no mistake, we are not fooling around here; an attempt has been made on Thea's life as well as Clark and me. You are here at the sufferance of Thea and I am the one who has kept this estate going for the last twenty-five years. You and Nigel have just sat around enjoying a life of luxury. I do not begrudge my brother's daughter her inheritance and I am proud I was able to keep the estate thriving even though you and Nigel spent money like it was going out of style. Enough! Tell us now where you were thirty minutes ago."

"We were right here together," screeched Prudence. "How dare you suggest such a thing?"

"Mother, please," Nigel said. "I don't want them to think we had anything to do with this either, but they must find out who is a threat to Thea. Can't you see how bad it looks for us? We have to cooperate with everyone. I know Sue thought I killed Tim, but I didn't. Tim let us have the run of the castle and I never cared about being the marquis anyway. I even warned Sue to watch out for danger, but I think she took it as a threat. I guess it might have sounded that way, but I was full of myself and my new title at the time. I am sorry. We truly were here all afternoon since lunch talking about what would happen to us if Thea turns us out. We haven't saved a farthing, don't you know. We are throwing ourselves at your mercy, Thea. Please let us stay here. I will help you all I can to find whoever is doing this to you."

"I haven't made any decisions about you and your family, Nigel, but common decency will allow you to stay for now. We must talk to all the servants here to verify your stories. Please tell them we are here to question them."

We talked to the cook and maid that lived at the dowager house and they both said that Nigel, Eileen and Prudence were in the garden after brunch until now. The cook couldn't clean up because they were dawdling about with the table and she was complaining to Freda, the maid, about it.

We returned to the castle to join the others in a very late lunch and it was very gloomy in the dining room.

"Everyone, please don't let this spoil your visit. Let's just go ahead and have fun like we planned. We will have a splendid dinner tonight and celebrate Mother's return to Tottersham. We are going to spend the rest of the day trying to place everyone that was at the castle. You can help by asking anyone you come in contact with where they were when the gargoyle fell in the garden. I am rather worried about you all and you might want to think about shortening your visit for now. I fear this is not over and I don't want any of you to get hurt."

Emmy jumped up and ran to put her arms around me. "Thea, I would never abandon you to danger. I for one am going to stay even if you tell me to go. The more people that are in the castle wandering around the more it may deter someone from trying again now that we are all on our guard."

The rest all chimed in with the same sentiment but Mr. Severied did say he would have to return to the states tomorrow. "I didn't intend to stay this long, Thea, but I must say I am very worried about you. Please be careful."

Sylvia and Arabella decided to go riding as the castle had a very nice stable with ten fine horses. Emmy and Bruce decided to stick around with Clark and me.

"Okay, Thea, who do you think is after you? I don't trust anyone here besides our group. We should think about where Colin could hide if he is the one that is after you," said Emmy.

"Perry is pretty sure that Colin isn't at the castle. I suppose he could be hiding somewhere. He knows the grounds like the back of his hand and it is very possible he is holed up in an outbuilding. We are going to look around ourselves as we don't know which of the hired help we can trust to search," I said.

We met Perry in the hall and he said he was going to enlist Herschel to help us. He said Herschel would know who could be trusted and they would make a thorough search. Herschel was waiting at the front of the castle and Perry introduced us to him.

"Mr. Dennis, I am so glad to meet you. My mother wrote about you and I thank you for helping Perry take care of all of the estate affairs for so many years."

"My pleasure, my lady. We aim to serve. Perry is a very able overseer. We will also take care of this little matter. Just leave it to us."

Clark said. "We are grateful for your expertise, Mr. Dennis, but this is a very serious matter. My wife's life depends on us getting to the bottom of this. Please be careful in what you divulge to others."

"Not to worry sir. We will be discretion itself. We are glad to have an active noble in the castle again."

Chapter 23

We waited for Perry to take care of a few errands and then the five of us set out to question the workers in the castle. We started at the top. The first person we encountered was Sandra coming out of the maids' quarters on the fourth floor. She was surprised to see the five of us and was immediately nervous.

Perry said, "Sandra, we are checking the whereabouts of everyone in the castle for this morning. Can you please tell us what you were doing from nine until twelve today?"

Sandra was promptly annoyed. "I was going about my duties Perry; with all the extra people in the castle we are all very busy. I can only say I was doing the rooms that the guests had used and didn't have time to check the clock. I was on the second, third and fourth floor all morning."

"Did you happen to see anyone acting suspicious?" asked Clark. "We are trying to pinpoint an incident and you could be a great help to us as you were on the spot so to speak. Can you tell us just who exactly you saw on these floors during your morning's work?"

"There are at least six maids that work these floors when we have guests and I saw them all at one time or another as I supervised their work. I am the head maid you know and I have to recheck their work. There was a good deal of activity on the upper floors today," she said.

"When was the last time you saw your son, Mrs. Pierce?" said Clark. "We are very anxious to know where he is."

Sandra bristled at once. "I know everyone tries to blame everything that happens around here on Colin. He is a good boy and has never caused any trouble in the castle. I haven't seen my son for at least twenty-five years. He was driven away by speculation that he pushed Lord Tim off the roof many years ago and he left with a broken heart. Lord Tim was his brother after all. He only wanted his rightful place in the castle and the archaic laws that prevented him from becoming Marquis after Lord Tim's death are not right. Lord Randall treated Colin and Perry just like Tim and we could only assume that the next oldest son would assume the title. It was a shock to find that Colin and Perry were not eligible to accede just because they were illegitimate. Randall loved them all equally. He educated them and gave them a place in his life. Doesn't it bother you, Perry, that you will never be recognized as an heir?"

"Not at all Sandra; all I ever wanted was to work for the estate. I was grateful I was given carte blanche to do as I pleased and to come and go as I pleased. I have done well and I am proud to say that the estate has thrived very well under my care. Thea will fare well thanks to my efforts and I don't begrudge her a thing. I was educated here in England with Tim and knew the laws of ascension while Colin chose American schools and didn't learn as much as he should have about royal dictates. I had no desire at any rate to be Marquis. My life is perfect just the way it is. You really have no idea where Colin is? I can't believe he hasn't got in touch with you for all these years," Perry said.

"He has not got in touch with me," Sandra said. "Now, I have work to do if you will excuse me."

She turned and walked down the hall with her head high. I felt sorry for her, but she had brought on her own problems.

We questioned the other six maids but the stories were all the same. Nobody paid much attention to everyday happenings and everyone was where they were supposed to be.

After questioning other various servants, we ended up in the kitchens with the cook and her helpers.

"Oh, my!" Mrs. Henderson said. "I am afraid my kitchens are a mess, my lady. I do apologize. I am preparing the evening meal. Whatever can I do for you?"

I looked at her spotless kitchens and her two well-turned-out helpers and smiled. "If it makes you more comfortable to call me by my title, you may do so. However, I am Thea to most people and you are welcome to call me that. We are here to ask a few questions about where everyone was this morning. We are hoping you or the girls can help us place people between nine and twelve today."

"Well, dear, we have all been right here in the kitchens all morning and the only people we saw were Perry and the two footmen, Charles and Harry. They were around to serve the meals with Molly my kitchen maid. Sarah and Beanie were right here with me. I wish we could help you. We were so shocked to hear about what happened this morning and glad you didn't have more than a few scratches. We do speculate among ourselves sometimes about Mr. Colin. I was here when Lord Tim died and it was a sad day for us all. He was a very good master. People talked about Mr. Colin being the evildoer, but I don't know. He was kind of a mild chap."

Clark said, "Have you seen Colin lately, Mrs. Henderson?"

"Oh no, the last time I saw Mr. Colin was about twenty-five years ago. He stopped in the kitchens to see me when he came to visit his mother. He was still pretty sad about Lord Tim and we chatted for a bit. He said he hadn't pushed Tim and he could prove it. He caught me up on his life. He had met a girl in school in America years ago; she came here to visit for a few days when he was in school and she met Lord Randall. Tim and Perry were still at their own schools at the time and did not meet her. They went back to America and they had gotten married. Something happened, because they weren't together anymore. He said he was going back to try and get back with his wife. He was still living off of his allotment that Lord Randall had given him for life, and he was just drifting around I guess. He didn't stay long. His poor mother misses him something dreadful. She has never been the same since Lord Tim died and Colin was suspected of the deed."

I said, "Thank you, Mrs. Henderson. We will all be in for dinner and Mr. Severied will be leaving first thing tomorrow. The others will be with us for a few more days anyway."

We took our leave and were going down to the stables when we heard a ruckus. Arabella and Sylvia appeared on the stable path in high dudgeon. It seems that Prudence was angry that they had taken her favorite horses for a run—she had been waiting to rant at them as they returned. Perry said, "Say no more, I will handle this." He disappeared in the direction of the stables and in a few minutes Prudence appeared and stormed in the direction of the dowager house.

"It would appear that some other arrangement will have to be made for Prudence and Nigel. She can't seem to get it through her head that she no longer has a say around here. I will talk to Mr. Severied and Granger tonight—they can come up with a solution," I said.

We returned to the castle and found Granger, Frank and Mr. Severied in the library enthusing over all the leather-bound legal books and histories. They were in their element and we all laughed that they were having such a good time perusing the wonderful treasures found there.

Sylvia and Arabella went to their rooms to tidy up for dinner and Clark and I sat down with the four lawyers to hash out a solution for the Warrens. They devised a plan where Nigel would receive a small allotment and a home far away from the castle and he would have to take responsibility for Prudence and Eileen. Feeling much better, I left the library with Clark. I am afraid I still harbored the resentment of Nigel being so heartless with my mother after my father's death.

Clark found Perry and the two of them left to visit the dowager house to tell the Warrens of their imminent departure. As soon as the legal papers were filed they would be gone. The men were fairly sure in their minds that Nigel and Prudence were not at fault for my father's death and we could dismiss them from the equation.

I went up to the master suite and when I opened the door, I found that the rooms had been totally ransacked. I wondered what someone had been looking for. All of the legal papers pertaining to my inheritance were well preserved with my father's solicitor and Mr. Severied. The only reason for this total mess was pure spite. My clothes were all tossed on the floor and Clark's papers were thrown all over the place. The drawers and closets had been emptied and the contents were strewn all over the floor. I rang for the maid and Sandra was at the door in a matter of minutes. She stood by the door in shock. I watched her carefully and though she seemed surprised I thought I detected a smirk on her face. She said she would make arrangements to have the room put to rights as soon as possible. She soon had her crew working hard. No real damage had been done, just someone making a point. Clark arrived just as they were finishing up and was totally disgusted. After the maids had finished, we started getting dressed for dinner. Our clothes had not been damaged, just thrown around. We determined to get to the bottom of it anyway.

We were just leaving the suite when my cell phone rang. Clark's rang at the same time. We both had world cells and could be reached anywhere. I answered my phone and my Uncle Hal spoke in an urgent tone. "Thea, I am so sorry to have to tell you that your little house has burned to the ground. I am so afraid Carry may have had something to do with it. The fire marshal is investigating right now. What should I do? Wanda is in hysterics and Carry is denying she ever went to your house. I don't want to believe this is happening. Can you please come home?"

Chapter 24

I looked at Clark and knew he was getting the same report from someone else and he had a very troubled look on his face.

"We will be there as soon as we can, Uncle Hal. Please stay calm and try to keep a lid on things until Clark can get there."

I closed up my phone and sat in a nearby chair. My legs were trembling and I wanted to cry. My beautiful little house; I loved it so much and now it was gone. Tears welled up in my eyes as Clark finished his conversation and rang off. He put his arms around me and said, "I am so sorry sweetheart; I know how much you loved your little house. We will go back and see what can be done."

"Could Colin have got back there and torched my house so quickly? Do we have two people who are trying to destroy me? Do you think Hillary would do such a thing? Uncle Hal told me she and Carry were palling around together; what if their anger fed each other to the point of this awful deed?"

"Let's wait until we find out what happened when we get home. That was the sheriff on the phone and we will get more info as soon as they have it. The fire marshal is pretty sure it was set by an amateur and he will have more for us later, too. Let's go down to eat and then we can get moving on getting home in a hurry."

We entered the dining room with such long faces that everyone knew at once that something was wrong.

"What happened?" Granger asked. "It must be serious."

"It is," said Clark. "We have to return to the states right away. Thea's house has burned to the ground. They suspect arson."

Everyone began talking at once. Sylvia said, "Oh Thea, not that beautiful Rigby House; is Mary all right?"

Emmy said, "No! It is your own little house, isn't it Thea? Anyone who knows you would know that would be the way to hurt you the most. I am so sorry sweetie."

I burst into tears at Emmy's understanding that the house was my own and my first mark of being a person in my own right.

She rushed over and gave me a hug as Sylvia and Arabella did the same.

Frank pulled out his phone and pushed a button. "Have the jet ready to go within the hour; we will be returning to the states at once." He closed his phone and we all began to make plans. As soon as we had finished eating we would pack and be on our way.

Perry came into the room and knew at once something was wrong. "What happened?"

Clark took him aside and told him what had happened. He crossed to my chair and lifted me up and held me for a minute. "I will make arrangements with Herschel and Mother and I can follow you in a couple of days." He left the room in a rush.

We all picked at the lavish meal Mrs. Henderson had prepared for us and after a few minutes I jumped up and said, "Let's get on with it; we are just wasting time picking at our food."

Within a half hour we were all in the limo that Frank had kept at the castle and headed to the airport. The plane was manned and ready and we took off almost immediately. We would arrive at Bangor sometime around eight o'clock p.m. American time. We all slept most of the way and when we arrived in Bangor, the men collected our various vehicles from long-term parking and we reversed our trip of a few days ago. It seemed like a month instead of a couple of days. Mr. Severied had made the trip with us again and had canceled his flight for the next day. We straggled into Trafton with our little convoy and Clark and I immediately went to the sheriff's office. Even though it was ten o'clock at night the sheriff was there and the place was humming.

"Have you found out any more since I talked to you?" Clark asked the sheriff.

"We are sure the fire was set. The dogs sniffed out the accelerant and we found a gas can in back near the woods. Whoever set the fire came through the woods. With Thea's house set back all by itself in the cul-de-sac, it was easy for someone to come right up to the house from the rear and splash the gas around. The neighbors didn't even notice until it was well involved. Their dog kept barking and finally they came out to look up the lane but by then it was too late. We have heard some scuttlebutt around town about Hillary Leighton and Carry Chadworth talking big about taking Thea down a peg or two. We talked with them both and they deny ever being at Thea's house. We are still checking their alibis. Hal is just sick about this. Victor Leighton is up in arms about us questioning his little princess of course. It could be just a couple of spoiled brats spouting off, but I wouldn't put it past them. Sorry, Thea. I know Carry is your cousin but she is traveling with Hillary and her fast crowd now and when they get drinking, hard telling what they will do."

Clark said, "Thanks, sheriff. I will have a talk with both of them. Maybe you scared them enough so they will be willing to talk. Let's get settled at my house for the night, Thea, and tomorrow we will get started on this investigation together."

We went to Clark's house and all was okay there. I was so glad that Emmy had taken the manuscripts back to the library safe. They would have been gone and they were the only true link to my mother. Everything else could be replaced, even though I loved everything about my little house. We were exhausted and quickly showered and got ready for bed. As we lay cuddling in bed, it finally hit me that my little home was gone and I sobbed into Clark's shoulder. He held me and said we would build another if I wanted it or I could do what I wanted to this cottage to make it mine. I finally fell to sleep only to dream.

In my dream, I was in the castle kitchen and Mrs. Henderson was saying, "Mr. Colin just traveled around living off his trust fund that Lord Randall had left him for life."

Chapter 25

I woke up early with the dream still fresh in my mind. I found Clark in the kitchen and he had been out and purchased groceries and had bacon and eggs ready for me. We sat down with our breakfast and munched toast and drank coffee along with our eggs and bacon. It was the best meal I had had in a long time—just the two of us in our own little home. I wasn't taking to the life of Lady Tottersham very well.

I told Clark about my dream. I said, "If we can find out who administers the trust to Colin we can find out where he is."

Clark said, "Good point, Thea. I'm sure Tim's solicitor either does that or knows who does."

"I am going to call him right now and find out," I said.

I went to the phone and called Mr. Severied and explained what I needed. He said he would get on it right away and get back to us with the information.

We decided we would talk to Carry first and headed to Wanda and Hal's house. Wanda answered the door and gave us a surly look and let us in with ill grace. Hal met us in the hall and welcomed us into his home and seated us in the parlor. When Clark told him we wanted to speak to Carry about the fire, Wanda shrieked that she should have her lawyer present. Hal said, "Wanda, for God's sake, stop it. This is Thea we are dealing with. Carry needs to come clean if she knows anything about that fire. Thea has lost her home and we need to help her."

"She has so many homes, why is that one a problem?" said Carry as she came sulking into the room.

"That little house meant more to me than any other place I will ever live," I said. "I bought it myself with money I had earned myself and I loved it. Please, Carry, if you know who burned it down, tell us now so we can get to the bottom of this whole thing."

"I told the sheriff that I didn't do it. Hillary and I have better things to do with our time than to bother about you Miss High and Mighty."

"That's enough, Carry," said Hal in a tight voice. "You will either help them and answer their questions, or you can leave this house right now. I am ashamed that you are my daughter."

"Hal!" screamed Aunt Wanda. "You can't do this. She is our daughter. What has gotten into you?"

"If I had spoken up years ago when you let her run roughshod over both of us and was mean to Thea, we wouldn't be in this mess. Now SHUT UP and Carry you better start talking NOW!" he shouted.

Carry looked at her father and decided she had pushed him as far as she could and began to talk. "We really didn't do it, Dad. We talked among ourselves about what we would like to do to Thea, but that wasn't one of them. She has everything and even took Clark away from Hillary and we were really pissed at her. She is a nobody and was raised by our family and look where she is, and look where we are."

Hal crossed the room and took Carry by the shoulders. "Don't you ever call my niece a nobody again. Do you hear me, Carry? She is the reason that we have what we have today. It was the money her mother gave us to keep her here with us that made it possible for you to sit around on your lazy arse and do nothing but cause trouble. Thea is not responsible for being an orphan; she is a victim of circumstance and she has turned out very well. I believe that is the influence that she got from my sister. For pity sakes, girl, smarten up and look around you. You have a nice home and a mother and father who love you. You don't need to turn a hand of work and you complain about someone who works hard. I believe that is the influence of that Leighton girl you have been hanging with. You always try to rise above yourself and I am sick of it. Either you accept who you are right now and live with it or go somewhere else and try to find a better deal." He turned to Clark. "For what it's worth, Clark, I think she is telling the truth. If it turns out she isn't then she can take whatever punishment that is coming to her. I wash my hands of her."

Carry ran from the room in tears with Wanda right behind her. Clark turned to Hal and said, "I think you are right Hal. I don't believe she had anything to do with the fire. If you have any say left at all, you should curb her time spent with Hillary. I have known Hillary since she was two, and she has always been spoiled. For the record, she and I were never an item. It was all in her head. She is just going to have to accept that Thea and I are together forever."

We parted from Uncle Hal on good terms and went to the Leighton house.

Chapter 26

The Leighton House was every bit as impressive as Granger and Sylvia's estate. It was hidden behind a large hedge and a gate overlooking the water.

Hillary answered the door before we could ring and waved off the butler who had just entered the hall. "Clark, darling, I see you have come to your senses. I always knew you would." She caught my movement from the side of the door and snarled. "What is she doing here?"

"Hillary, Thea is my wife. I love her with all my heart. She will always be my wife. Get that through your head and you will be much happier with yourself. We never had anything going other than to partner at a few parties that our mothers put on. I can barely tolerate you if the truth be known and never could. Now, I would like to ask you some questions about the fire on Wheaten Road. You can answer them here or you can accompany us down to the sheriff's department and answer them there."

"I don't have to let her in. I hate her and she has no right to be here."

Clark said, "She is my deputy and has every right to ask questions." He said this with a straight face and Hilllary didn't argue the point. She just determined to be even more of a bitch. She took us into the den and sat without inviting us to do the same. Clark merely waved me to a seat and sat in the chair beside me.

"Now, where were you when Thea's house burned? I'd advise you to cooperate and tell me the truth if you have it in you, Hillary," he said.

Hillary glared at both of us and said, "I didn't burn that bitch's house down. I was with friends all last night. Carry and I talk about what we would like to do to her, but it is just talk. We can't be bothered," she sneered.

"Like you couldn't be bothered to shred her gloves and wrap the night of the Vermillion reception?"

"You can't prove I did that," she screamed.

"I would advise you to calm down, Hillary. You are really at the mercy of Thea as someone has come forward to tell me that you did indeed slash her clothes. You were seen and the cost of those items adds up to a felony. That means jail time, Hillary, now come clean about the fire."

"I didn't do it, Clark, I swear. I'm afraid of fire and we never even discussed fire anyway."

"What did you discuss, Hillary? Bear in mind I have already talked with Carry."

"We were only talking, we never would have done anything to your little precious, it just made us feel better to vent about it. If Carry said otherwise she is a liar."

Clark gave her a piece of paper and told her to write down who she was with at the time of the fire and she scribbled a few names down and slammed out of the room. We let ourselves out as the butler nodded from the staircase.

We then drove over to Wheaten Street where my little house used to be. There was nothing but the foundation left. We sat a long time and just looked at the result of someone's total hate for me and we both shuddered.

We left and went to the Bell, a seafood restaurant, and had a nice lunch. We didn't talk about the fire by mutual agreement. Just as we finished eating, my phone rang. It was Mr. Severied. He said that Arnold Holt, my father's solicitor, had told him that ever since Colin left the castle after Father's death he always had his checks sent to the same bank account in Boston. They always came back as received by the bank and he supposed that Colin used that account from all over the world. That is all he could tell him. I thanked him and we hung up.

Clark and I discussed the possibility of staking out the bank, but decided that Arnold was right and Colin could be anywhere in the world and still draw on that account. The police really had no reasonable cause to get a warrant to search the account for clues to his whereabouts. Clark said he would think on it. The afternoon fled and we were no further ahead.

I suddenly remembered that we should check on Mary. She was all alone at Rigby House and if someone wanted to harm me they might go there to wreak havoc. We left Trafton, drove through Rigby, and went the last five miles to Rigby House holding our breaths. We expected to see smoke at any time. We arrived just after seven o'clock and the house was dark. It wasn't dark outside yet but still there should have been lights on somewhere in the house.

Clark left the car right on the drive and I let us in with my key. Everything was quiet as the grave. I went to my study and saw that the lock had been tampered with, but the lock was solid and short of a bomb it could not be picked.

We rushed to the kitchen area and Mary's suite. It was very quiet. Mary was nowhere around. Her apartment was closed up and the door was locked.

"Do you have a key to this door?" Clark asked.

"Yes, it is in my study. There is a panel that holds all the keys except the study itself." I rushed back to the study to get the key.

We let ourselves into Mary's apartment to see if she was all right. It was empty of all life including the plants on the windowsill. For the first time we noticed that the house was dusty and probably hadn't been cleaned for a few days, probably since we had been in England. We began to search her apartment for clues as to where she could be. Her desk was in the corner of the living room and she had left it open. I sat down in her chair and began to look for a note or anything that might tell us if she had left by herself. An angry voice said, "I should have known you would be just like your mother, sticking your nose into my business."

Chapter 27

Clark and I turned to see Mary advance into the room with a furious look on her face.

"What are you doing searching my place?" she yelled. "I am entitled to my privacy. You have no right to search my things."

"I am sorry for opening your door and looking for a clue as to where you were, Mary," I said. "We were worried about you. My house in Trafton was burned to the ground with arson and we thought you might be in danger. I didn't know you would be gone."

"Well, you all left at the drop of a hat without telling me where you were going so I thought I would just take a couple days off. That doesn't give you the right to go through my things, so leave my suite at once!"

"Mary, we will leave of course, but you don't have to be so angry. We weren't poking into anything. We will be upstairs when you calm down and I would like to know what you meant by me being just like my mother. I think that deserves an explanation."

Mary slammed the door of her apartment behind us and we went up to my bedroom to discuss this latest development.

"What do you suppose she is hiding?" asked Clark. "She is guilty of something for sure. Maybe I need to take another look at our Mary."

"I can't believe she was so angry at us. We were just trying to see if she was all right."

"Maybe she just didn't like to be caught taking time off and letting the house go without asking," Clark said.

"What did she mean about Mother?" I asked. "She made it sound like she hated my mother. Do you think she could have hurt her?"

"Before today, I would have said no, but now I am not so sure. Like I said, I think I will take another look."

The front door slammed and I went to the window to see where Mary was going. She was opening the door to a beautiful metallic blue Chrysler convertible. She reached in and pulled out her two bags and brought them back into the house. It was apparent by her movements that she was still steaming.

"Where did she get that car?" I asked. "I pay her well and she doesn't have to spend it on anything but herself, but she usually drives the house wagon. Why would she need a car?"

"Maybe she just wanted something to call her own," Clark said "You can understand that."

"That I can," I said.

There was a tap on the door and Mary opened it when I said to come in. She came in very meekly and looked at me with red eyes. "I need to explain about Sue," she said. "Sue was very nosy and wouldn't let me have any privacy. She had to know everything. I even caught her looking at my personal mail. Please accept my apology and let us get back to normal. I need to start cleaning the house now. It is very dusty from my absence." I just looked at her and she turned and left the room.

Clark laughed and said, "As apologies go that was a loser. Was your mother a prier?"

"No," I said. "She never entered my room without permission and Perry and Mary had the run of the place. She never asked them for an explanation of any kind and she certainly would not go through anybody's private mail. I wonder why Mary would say such a thing."

"Well, let's go back to my house for the night. I don't want to stay here," Clark said.

"I'll tell Mary we are leaving. I need to lock the study and we can be on our way."

I went down the stairs and down the hall to my study. Mary was just coming out. "I was just seeing if it needed to be dusted in there," she said. I looked at her and stepped around her. The box that I had left on the chair was on the desk and had been pawed through in a hurry. "Did you find what you were looking for, Mary?" I asked.

"Now you know how I felt," she said. She started to walk toward the kitchen. "Mary, wait." I said. She turned around and looked at me with hate. "What is the matter with you?" I cried. "We have known each other for years and now you act like you hate me; what have I done to make you feel this way?"

"You should know. The way you have been putting on airs since you picked up your title. Well, you aren't the only one who deserved that title, are you?"

"What do you know about heirs to my title, Mary? What makes you think there are others and why do you care? What difference does it make to you?"

Clark had come into the hall and was watching Mary with surprise on his face. He couldn't be any more surprised than I was.

It was like touching a match to gasoline. "What difference does it make to me?" she screeched. "I'll tell you what difference it makes to me. I am married to Colin Pierce and he should have inherited the title, not you. He is the rightful heir and I should be living in the castle at Shea. You and your meddling mother ruined everything. First she comes to the castle and marries Tim at the drop of a hat and threatens to produce a direct heir. Then when Tim is dead she still manages to screw us over. That fag inherited everything and he wasn't even a close relative to Lord Randall. Just when we think he will die without an heir and Colin will inherit, then you surface and claim it all. I hate you. I have all I can do to stay in the same house with you." She sputtered to a stop seething with anger.

Chapter 28

I must have had my mouth open and certainly was lost for speech when Clark spoke in a gentle voice from behind Mary. "Where is Colin, Mary? We would like to talk with him."

She spun around in surprise. "Ha!" she screamed. "You will never find him—not until I am good and ready to tell you where he is, and that will be never."

"How did you meet Colin, Mary?" Clark asked. His voice was so gentle that she seemed to respond to him.

"We met at college in Boston. His father had let him choose whatever school he wanted to attend and he came over to Boston. I had gone down to Boston to college and it was love at first sight. He told me all about being heir to the title of Marquis of Tottersham and we got married after a short time. He said I would someday be the Marchioness of Tottersham. We went over to England and I met his mother and Lord Randall; that was before he died. We were planning to go back over to England and be with his family after the baby was born. Colin was with his mother when Lord Tim was killed. I was pregnant and the doctor told me not to travel so Colin had gone by himself to see his mother. He was immediately immersed in a legal struggle because he was not Randall's legitimate son. He lost the title and was left with just the allotment that his father had arranged for him. He came back to Boston and told me we would never have the castle. I flew into a rage and very soon after I lost our baby and Colin left me. He went back to see his mother after traveling for a while and then he decided to come back to me. I told him I didn't ever want to see him again and he left. I get a post card from time to time and never gave up hope that he would be with me again and we would inherit the castle. It was pure coincidence that brought me to Sue Chadworth's house and I didn't know she was Lady Tottersham until just before she died. I came back to Trafton to see my mother and saw the ad in the paper. I didn't use my married name when Sue hired me as the Ameses are well known around here."

"Did you poison Sue, Mary?" Clark could see she was in a delicate mental state and spoke so lightly I could hardly hear him.

She sat down in a chair in the hall. She put her head in her hands. "I was tired of living here with no life. At first it was restful with no real responsibilities and everything paid for and the years just flew by. I had Perry for company and he was pleasant and then Sue brought that little orphan girl that was living with Hal, and she was so cute that she reminded me of the child I had lost. We all rubbed along nicely. One day I dropped a bank statement by mistake and Sue opened it by mistake. She saw that the inside was addressed to Colin Pierce. His statements always came to me here. He didn't mind. Anyway, Sue confronted me just after Perry left for his vacation. She thought that I was spying on her for Colin. She told me to work my two weeks and then leave. On the last day just before Perry was to come home, I asked her if she wanted me to prepare lunch before I left. She said no but I put the nicotine in her drink when she left it to go upstairs for a minute. It didn't take long for her to die and then I dragged her up to the third floor and dropped her off the roof. I then cleaned everything up, emptied her study and room of all personal stuff and put it all in the cubby. I left and waited for Perry to come and find the body. I intended to go through the stuff from the study later, but the place was like a zoo. I never got the chance to see if she had written anything down about me and kept trying to get the chance to see. Then Miss Nosy there found all the stuff and locked it in the study again with a new lock. Then the little slut took up with you in the blink of an eye and I was really stymied—like mother, like daughter.

"When you all tore out of town, I figured you had gone to England and thought it would be a good time to make some plans of my own. First I drove into town and went through the woods to Thea's house. I took some of Perry's stuff in the shed and used it to set her house on fire. I figured if there were any prints on the can of gas and rags they would come back to Perry. Don't think I didn't know he had taken up with Sue before he left for vacation—serves him right.

"I had all of the money that had collected in Colin's account for over twenty-five years and decided to have some fun of my own. I bought a new car and rented an apartment in Boston. I am leaving as soon as I pack my bags I brought back with me. You can all get stuffed."

I didn't know Clark had called the sheriff's department, but they had heard it all on his cell and before Mary could even cross the hall the front door burst open and the sheriff and two deputies assisted Clark with putting a wild and crazy Mary in cuffs and into a squad car. She tried to kick out the windows of the back seat as they continued on to the state hospital in Bangor where she was given a sedative and fell asleep from exhaustion.

Later that night after we had closed up Rigby House soundly, we were at the sheriff's department speculating with Sheriff Jordan about what Mary had done with Colin. It only stood to reason that she must have killed him too as she had access to his money and he hadn't got in touch with his mother since the last time he was in England and he said he was coming back to his wife. Maybe the doctors could get her to talk about it.

The mystery about who killed my mother was solved, but what about my father?

Chapter 29

Clark and I decided that we would stay in Trafton for a while and I called Emmy the next day to fill her in. She was flabbergasted at Mary's involvement.

"But she couldn't have killed your father," she said. "How are we going to find out who did?"

"Clark and I will be staying here for a while and don't worry, the investigation will continue."

I asked her if she had been to the library and she said that Temple had been amazing. She had everything under control.

"Everything, that is, except her temper—at Andrew Vermillion. I walked in to find her telling him to leave the library and never to come back. She was wild. He always did tease her beyond reason and I guess he had gone too far. She even threw a magazine at him." Emmy laughed.

"Oh, that's too bad. I hope they settle their differences," I said.

"They have always had a contentious relationship. She has always had to work so hard for everything and she said he was just a spoiled brat rich kid. They will either kill each other or love each other. We'll have to wait and see. How is everybody else? Did Granger and Sylvia find everything okay when they returned?"

"Clark checked in with everybody this morning and they are all tired but happy to be home I guess. They are shocked of course about Mary. Clark is going to try to talk to her again. He is going to see her at the hospital today if her doctors will allow him."

"To think that you ate her cooking and were alone with her—she could have killed you at any time."

"She had no idea I was related to Tim or Sue. Remember she had never met Tim so she didn't know how much I looked like him. When she found out I was Tim's daughter she had to act calm, but inside she was seething," I said.

"Well, let me know what is happening. Will you be coming back to the library now?"

"No, Perry will be home soon and we need to do something about Rigby House. I leave the library in your capable hands along with Temple and you can referee her and Andrew."

Chapter 30

Clark arrived at the mental hospital around two o'clock and the doctors said it might do Mary good to talk with him. He entered her room in a calm manner and said hello to her as if he was just coming for a nice visit.

"Hello, Mary, so nice to see you again. I wonder if you might help me with a few questions I have. I know you are the only person who can help and I sure would appreciate any assistance you can give me."

Mary looked at him with a calm expression and asked him to have a seat.

"Can we start from the beginning, Mary?" he asked. "Can you tell me all about Colin and how you met and the life you had together?"

Mary smiled at him and said, "We met for the first time when Colin came to America to attend the same college that I was attending in Boston. We took one look and clicked. He was rich and I was poor but he didn't care. He asked me to move into his apartment and I did. We were so in love. He told me all about the title he was going to have and we would live in a castle. I should have known that Mary Ames from Trafton, Maine, was not going to be a Marchioness. He even took me to Shea in Britain and I met his father and mother. They were both very kind to me. We were married when we came back to the states. Randall and Sandra even came to the wedding. Then his father died and Tim took over the title. Colin said it wouldn't last long as Tim was very reckless and was too much of a womanizer to settle down. We lived together for a couple of years and Colin would visit his mother from time to time. He was visiting her when Tim was killed and I was very pregnant. He thought that he would get the title right then and there but they told him he could never inherit as he was illegitimate. He left in a fury and only went back once. I had lost the baby soon after he told me we would never live in the castle and he left me. I had the baby buried; it was a little girl. I named her Charlotte. He went to England to visit his mother to tell her he hadn't killed Tim and then he came back to me. I was glad to see him and said that someday he could still inherit as his cousin or whoever was gay and would get aids and die. He said I didn't understand. He could never inherit as he was illegitimate. I was cooking breakfast and was so angry I hit him with a fry pan and he fell down and never got back up. I found some old clothes and scruffed him up a bit to make him look homeless and when it got dark, I took him out and dropped him in an alley. The next day they said they had found a homeless man in an alley and he had fallen and hit his head. They buried him in an unmarked grave as an unknown. I closed up the apartment and told the bank to forward our statements to me with Colin's name inside as he was out of the country right then. Colin was very generous and had added me to his account. I have saved the money ever since. I have hundreds of thousands of dollars in the bank. I am a very important woman. I am very clever don't you think, Lieutenant Sanderson?"

"You are very clever, Mary," Clark said. "Do you know who might have killed Lord Tim in England?"

"I think that sneaky cousin of his killed Tim just so he could inherit. They always blamed my Colin but he wouldn't hurt a flea. My Colin was very special. His mother used to say that, too. My Colin is very special."

Clark thanked Mary and took his leave. The doctors said she probably never would stand trial as she was totally out of touch with reality. Clark agreed.

Chapter 31

Clark arrived back in Trafton early that evening and shared his report with me. We felt bad for both Mary and Colin, but we felt worse for Sue and Tim. I was depressed and feeling very frustrated.

My phone rang and it was Perry. He was at Rigby House and it was all closed up. Where was Mary? What had happened? I filled him in and he was absolutely shocked. Colin was dead? Mary was insane? What about Tim? What about Rigby House?

I told him that Clark and I would be right out and we would bring some pizzas for supper. Perry said he would clean up in his apartment and be waiting for us. We went right to his apartment when we arrived at Rigby House and we shared both pizza and our story with him. He was amazed.

"I will have to call my mother so she can tell Sandra that Colin is dead. She deserves to know after all these years," Perry said.

"Yes. I am going to get in touch with Boston's coroner's office and see about trying to find the pauper's grave where Colin is buried. We can arrange to have him sent back to Shea if we can find him," said Clark.

"Oh, Clark, do you think they will be able to locate the grave?" I asked.

"Sometimes they keep really great records in case someone comes along years later looking for a loved one. We can only try."

Clark and I decided to stay at Rigby House for the night and we left Perry to make his call. The house gave off a feeling of loneliness when we entered the front hall.

"We must decide what to do with this house and how we are going to manage between here and Shea," I said.

"Plenty of time for that darling when we have less to think about; right now I want to search Mary's apartment and see if there are any clues at all as to where Colin is buried and what happened to him."

"Let's do it then. I will get the key."

We entered Mary's suite with some trepidation. We expected her to jump out at us at any time and accuse us of snooping at any time. It was just as we had left it and we resumed the search we had started the last time we were here.

I opened the top drawer to Mary's desk and found her bank statements for the last twenty five years. She had kept them all. The money from Colin's allowance had just kept coming and she had spent very little of it. There was no doubt in our minds that he was dead. The last time Colin himself had made a withdrawal was about the time he came back from England for the last time after talking with Mrs. Henderson at the castle kitchen. Mary had withdrawn quite a lot recently and her purse was sitting on the study window seat. We looked in her purse and found quite a bit of cash and the records for her new car and receipts for quite a wardrobe. We would have to follow up on the apartment she had rented and dispose of her stuff. What a mess.

Randall had been very generous with his son and over the last twenty six or so years the account had amassed over two and a half million plus interest. Clark whistled at the amount and asked, "What happens to the money now?"

"I don't know. It really belongs to the Tottersham estate as Colin was not the beneficiary. The money was supposed to stop at his death. I suppose it could go toward helping pay for Mary's care at the hospital even though she doesn't deserve our help. I will ask Perry and Mr. Severied to handle this part of the case as I am still at a loss as to what to do—Perry is very familiar with all of that. He and Herschel have kept the estate fluid and prosperous for all these years and I don't see any sense in changing that, do you?"

"That sounds like the sensible thing to do right now," Clark said. "What else is here anyway? Let's look further."

Mary had lived very frugally for a rich woman. Maybe she felt guilty about using the money for herself. There were no records or diaries of any kind, so it was all going to stay locked up in Mary's febrile mind I guess.

Chapter 32

The next day we got an early start. We really didn't have to go anywhere so we could begin on our inquiries as soon as places of business opened.

Perry came to the kitchen as we were finishing up a light breakfast. He sat with us for a cup of coffee and we told him about the money. He said that Randall had settled that amount on the boys when they had left school and of course Tim had got the whole enchilada. "I have invested my share of my father's estate and I am a rich man by any standards I guess. I have always had this job in Maine, my salary from the estate as well as my allowance and my needs have been few. My mother is in her sixties and she is so happy running the castle day to day events that she will never retire. Sandra is about the same age and she has indicated she will never give up her post either. Mother said she would tell Sandra about Colin and be sure she was taken care of."

We discussed what we would each do and Perry said he would take care of stopping the allowance at the bank and talk with Mr. Severied about getting the money back to the estate coffers. He said he thought that the estate should cover Mary's medical bills and would see to that as well.

Clark went to my study and immediately got busy talking with the coroner's office in Boston. He explained what the circumstances were and they said they thought they could help with the search. Their records were very comprehensive and they would get back to him.

I intended to get a start on what I was going to do with the estate and Rigby House. I sat in the kitchen and looked out the window at the bay. I would never sell Rigby House but I needed a staff to be here while we were gone. I needed to get in touch with a staffing agency and have those needs met at once. I talked with Perry about what he wanted to do and he said that he would be glad to supervise a staff that could handle the Rigby property while we were away at various times. He would need to be flexible with all the estates. I gave him my blessing to do what he thought best and he left to get a start with Mr. Severied. I phoned a reputable staffing agency and told them what we needed. They said it would take a few days to recruit a crew and they would get back to us for interviews.

As I was leaving the kitchen the phone rang. It was Clara. She said that she had tried Perry's apartment and thought she might reach him at the house. I told her that he was not here right now and she said she wanted us to know that she had broken the news to Sandra.

"I told her Mary was in the state hospital and not doing well. She just stood there for a few minutes and then she said she always knew that he was dead. He would never not get in touch with her for all those years if he was alive. Then she turned around and started to leave, then stopped and said she would be leaving the castle for a while. She just left with several bags for London and said she didn't know when she would be back. I guess she has had enough after all these years," Clara said.

I thanked Clara for calling and told her I didn't know when we would be seeing her again but to keep the home fires burning. She laughed and said she would. She was as jolly as Sandra was dour.

Clark went back to Trafton to the sheriff's office and I called Emmy for lunch. She said we could meet at The Gull restaurant in Trafton and we made plans for noon.

Emmy had already ordered for us when I arrived. It was a good thing she did because the restaurant was crowded with tourists and it was loud. Emmy had ordered one of my favorites from The Gull, haddock sandwich with limeade. It was yummy. We ate quickly and left for some peace and quiet at the library.

We helped Temple with a line of patrons and then went into my office. Emmy and Temple had not disturbed my things, but had merely added theirs. It was a large office with a couch and two stuffed chairs beside the desk and file cabinets. The safe was in the wall behind the desk. We sat down in the chairs and sighed. We talked about Mary and I told Emmy how Sandra had simply left the castle when she heard about Colin; we agreed that it was a pity. I left around five o'clock to go back to Rigby House as Clark would be home at six. Good wife that I was I picked up take-out salads and burgers in Rigby and Clark was already home when I got there. We shared with Perry as I had gotten enough for him, too, and we compared our busy day.

Chapter 33

I told Perry that his mother had called and what she had to say. Both Clark and Perry were surprised that Sandra would leave the castle. Perry said she had only taken a vacation once and that was to see Colin at school in America when he graduated from college. She had gone with Randall. She came back from her trip just glowing. She really thought that Randall was going to marry her.

Clark said, "Well, the coroner's office is very efficient. They already have a lead on the grave site and are going to continue with that search. They will get back to me when they know more. It will probably take a few weeks."

"Great news, darling," I said. "I also was busy. I called the staff agency and they are compiling a list for us to interview for our needs here." I grinned. "A cook would help."

Clark and Perry both chuckled and we felt as if we were going to be happy for the first time. I told them that I wanted to keep Rigby House open and live here for now. Clark said that he liked that idea. Perry said that was good news for him, too, as he really liked the house and grounds.

"Over the years as I grew closer to Sue, I felt that this was my true home. I really loved her and we probably would have been married if she had lived. I don't think Tim would have minded, Thea."

"From what she wrote in her journals, I think you are right, Perry. I would like to get to know you better this summer, too," I said.

Perry cleared his throat and left to go back to his place.

Clark and I just sat in the parlor and snuggled while we talked about how we would spend the summer.

"I am swamped at the sheriff's department and really need to put in some time catching up with my different cases. Do you mind darling?" Clark asked.

"No, I really want to spend the next couple of months just relaxing and being with Perry to get to know more about both my mother and father. I am so fortunate that he knew both of them so well. He can tell me so much about them. He and I will be busy the next couple of weeks choosing a staff for this place. Do you want some input on who we hire, Clark?"

"No, I trust your judgment and Perry is an expert at these things from what I understand from Herschel. You two go ahead and I am sure everything will fall into place."

We both decided we would very much like to spend some time in bed tonight so we retired to our room. We would have to do something about changing our quarters but that could wait for now.

Chapter 34

We settled into a routine over the next couple of days and I shopped for groceries and did the best I could to feed us. Clark would leave promptly at eight o'clock unless he had been called out in the night and he usually made it home while his meager supper was still hot. Neither man complained about my cooking and I was grateful for that.

Three days later the staffing agency sent us our first batch of applicants and Perry took the day off to help me interview them. We had decided that we needed a cook/chef that could handle lavish meals for entertaining, a cleaning woman that would come in daily from outside, and a factotum that could train under Perry and handle all the duties, both in and outside the house. We soon discovered that on the coast of Maine these talented people were plentiful and over the course of the next two days we interviewed dozens of people and finally settled on the same candidates. We were surprised that we gravitated to the same people and didn't have any differences of opinion at all.

Our new chef was Rene Grenier, a graduate of a famous Boston culinary school and a favorite of the restaurants in the area. He was thirtyish with dark hair and dark eyes. He wanted to be able to create at his leisure with no expenses spared and found that he liked the idea of cooking for a private estate instead of working in a seasonal business like the coastal community offered. He settled into Mary's suite of rooms quite happily.

Tardy Burger was a real find and Perry was very impressed with the young handyman, chauffer, boatman. He had previously worked for a famous artist who had lived in Trafton seasonally, but whose health had failed to the point of a nursing home and Tardy wanted to work an active estate where his talents could be appreciated. Tardy was around thirty also and had a girlfriend that he was serious about so he wanted to be able to settle down in permanent employment. Her name was Gretchen Fuller and she tentatively asked if she could be interviewed for the housekeeping position. Perry and I were delighted to find she was just what we were looking for. She could come in every day to do what needed to be done and I would have a list of duties, if any, that she could do in addition. She would clean and wash up after Rene and do the laundry once or twice a week. I told her I realized it was a huge house and that I would hire the same team that used to do the heavy cleaning for my mother, such as carpets, floors, windows, etc.

We were all set for personnel. Tardy asked if we would have a problem with Gretchen living with him in Perry's apartment and we both said absolutely not. The apartment extended over the entire four-car garage and shop and was actually quite nice. It had two bedrooms, living room, eat-in kitchen and huge bathroom with a hot tub on a deck that Perry had created. They were as happy as we were. Gretchen also had several friends that would be glad to help out if we entertained. It was a winning situation for us all.

Of course I had finally finagled Perry into moving into the main house with Clark and me and we then got started on renovations on suites for both of us. Time flew like the wind and Perry and I actually had a wonderful time making plans. We were lucky enough to get one of the best contractors on the coast and we made arrangements for him to start immediately.

We decided the downstairs would be community and we all shared that equally—except for my study—and since both Perry and Clark needed a study of their own, we would use two large sitting rooms overlooking the water on the back of Rigby House and make them each a beautiful study. There was still the library, parlor, front sitting room, another back sitting room, large formal dining room and of course the kitchen area with Mary's suite and laundry rooms. The full cellar held a well-stocked wine room with controlled temperature. And a full recreation room that was open for all to use and we all did regularly. A large deck opened off the back terrace and a large rectangular swimming pool was situated there. It was used regularly as well.

The second floor would retain many bedrooms and baths, but several would be turned into a luxury suite for Clark and me. Perry sketched beautifully and he had designs for it all including a full nursery. The third floor was ditto only Perry would have his own quarters and he had a ball designing a full apartment for himself. It was beautiful.

The tower room with the cupola, of course, was mine. No renovations needed. Perry totally understood. My study was left open to all and I put mother's manuscripts that Mary had crammed into the cubby on a special shelf waiting for me to have the time to deal with them.

Time passed and Mr. Severied arrived one day to tell Perry and me that the money had been returned to the Tottersham estates and that arrangements had been made to pay Mary's hospital bills. She had been deemed incompetent to stand trial at this time. The doctors were working with her and she was improving every day. He said she had a regular visitor that seemed to cheer her up and they talked for hours. We all speculated on who it could be. She must have had friends after all.

Chapter 35

Clark finally got a call from the Boston coroner's office and they had found a body that they thought was Colin Pierce. Clark asked and received permission from a judge for exhumation and hoped that they would be able to get enough DNA after all those years to test for identification. Clark asked Perry if he would mind giving a DNA sample and he gladly submitted one. They said it would take several weeks again.

I suddenly thought about Mary's child. Where was the baby buried? That child should have a decent burial too. I needed to talk to Mary. Maybe she could tell us where the baby was. I turned to Clark and said, "I need to go to Bangor to see Mary. I need to find out what she did with her baby. That baby needs a decent burial and I want to do it."

"I don't like that idea, Thea," he said. "What if she turns violent again? I don't want you to take that chance."

"Clark, this is something I need to do. I was a baby that was separated from my family through no fault of my own and I want to make it right and put Randall's grandchild in the family crypt with her father."

"I can't let you go alone. Perry, will you go with her? I know that Mary killed Sue, but we must protect Thea and I can't get away right now. Thea is so set on this I am afraid for her."

"I will go with her for sure. I would like to talk with Mary about my brother too; this will give me the chance."

Clark said, "Thea, are you sure you need to do this? Can't you wait until I can go with you?"

"Clark, I love you with all my heart and I won't take any risks. Perry will be with me and I want to talk with Mary's friend also. Please say you understand."

"Darling, I understand but it won't make me worry any less. When are you leaving?"

"Perry and I are at a standstill here. We have instructed everyone what we want and it is up to the builders now. I would like to leave first thing in the morning."

We left at six in the morning. Rene had taken it all in stride and even packed us a lunch with cold drinks and coffee.

I laughed. "We are just going to Bangor, Rene, but this will surely come in handy. Thank you very much."

Perry was a great driver and he knew the route well having traveled it so many times in his travels to the airport. We made good time and arrived at the hospital just before eight o'clock. We sat in the car and enjoyed the coffee that Rene had packed. Perry had regaled me with stories of my father as a child and I laughed so hard I cried. We were growing very close as relatives and I was so glad to have another uncle.

Chapter 36

When it was after eight we went to the receptionist and asked if we might talk with Mary Ames.

The receptionist looked surprised and asked what relation we were to her. I explained that we were her brother-in-law and her niece. The woman acted flustered and called a doctor to the front.

"Is there a problem with our seeing Mary, doctor?" I asked.

"I understand that you are her niece and brother-in-law," he said. "I have intended to put in a call to Deputy Sanderson this morning. Mary died under extenuating circumstances last night and we haven't been able to determine the cause of her death yet, but I have to tell you I suspect foul play. She was perfectly okay when I saw her at four o'clock rounds and was laughing with her friend. The lady was quite a bit older than Mary, but they seemed to get along famously."

"Do you know what her name is?" I asked.

"No, I didn't much bother with the introduction; busy you understand. It wasn't her family from Trafton as they had disowned her, or so she said."

"Do you have sign-in sheets?" I asked.

"Oh yes, Lisa can help you with that. I need to call Lieutenant Sanderson and let the other authorities know of her death."

"I am Mrs. Sanderson and I can assure you that the Lieutenant will want to know everything that transpires about Mary and her mysterious visitor and her death. What time did she die? Why wasn't the Lieutenant called last night?"

"Oh, I didn't know you were the Lieutenant's wife," he said. "Lisa, will you please get Mrs. Sanderson the sign-in sheets on Mary Ames?" he called to the receptionist.

"Certainly Doctor Farley," she said.

Lisa rummaged around under the counter and pushed a clipboard toward me. The visitor had signed in under the name J. Jones and she was a very frequent visitor.

"Mrs. Jones was very nice and Mary liked her a lot. They always kissed each other on the cheek," Lisa said.

I called Clark immediately and explained what Dr. Farley had said about Mary. Clark said, "Let me speak to Farley, Thea. Thank you darling." I handed the phone to Dr. Farley and Clark proceeded to burn his ear. The doctor stammered a few sentences and handed the phone back to me.

"Thea, please stay there in the lobby and talk with a friend of mine with the Bangor Police. He will be there shortly. That fool Farley has probably destroyed all the evidence both in the room and on the body. I will be there as soon as I can. I am coming by helicopter. I love you babe."

I turned to Perry with a bemused look on my face.

"Clark wants us to stay here. A friend from the Bangor Police will be here shortly and he needs us to fill them in on what has happened prior to this."

"Dr. Farley," I said, "the Lieutenant wants you to be available to the Bangor Police who are arriving shortly and the Lieutenant is flying in himself. Please stop anyone from going near the room and the body if you haven't already removed it from the premises; if you have, call them and tell whomever you speak to that this is a police matter and to leave the body as it is until the police arrive."

I turned to Lisa as I heard sirens come into the hospital lot. "Would you happen to have anything that Mrs. Jones touched?" I asked.

"Oh, you mean for fingerprints?" Lisa asked. "Clever, Mrs. Sanderson, but she always wore gloves. She was a real lady, kind of regal."

Perry and I exchanged glances. "What did she look like?" Perry said.

"She was about seventy I would say; a well-preserved seventy, she always had her hair just so and wore pretty suits and gloves with nice pumps to match. She was about your height, Mrs. Sanderson. She left just before eight last night and they found Mary dead shortly after."

The door burst open and an officer about Clark's age strode into the lobby. He held his hand out to me and said, "I'm Paul Decker. Clark and I went to the academy together. I didn't even know he was married."

I introduced Perry to Officer Decker and filled him in on what had happened. "You will want to talk with Lisa here. She is very sharp and will be a big help."

He raised his eyebrows and said, "No nonsense, just like Clark."

"Clark will be here very shortly, he is flying in by helicopter. He asked that you preserve what is left of the scene and make sure that the body is as untouched as possible. I have an idea as to who the mystery woman is that left her shortly before her death."

Perry had whipped out his cell phone as soon as Lisa described the mystery woman. He now crossed the room to where I stood talking to Paul Decker. "Let's show this to Lisa and see if she can identify the woman." He took his phone to Lisa and asked her if she recognized the woman in the picture.

"Yes, that is Mrs. Jones," she said excitedly. Paul Decker asked Lisa if she could run off some copies from Perry's phone and she said sure. Perry and I told Paul about Sandra Pierce and that she was the "Mrs. Jones" in the picture. When Lisa returned with the phone and several dozen copies, Paul Decker began distributing them to his men. "She can't be far. Check the car rental agencies to see if Mrs. J. Jones rented a car and what kind.

"She may possibly have bought one," I said. "She is very affluent and could afford to pay cash for one."

"Check the cab companies, too," said Paul.

His men scattered in all directions and Paul Decker collared the good doctor and they went to Mary's room.

Clark had landed his helicopter on the heliport of another large hospital and a squad car had picked him up. It was within minutes of the state hospital and he was soon with us. He kissed me and shook hands with Perry and we told him about Sandra being identified as the mystery woman.

"I'd better look to my laurels." He laughed and disappeared down the hall to Mary's room.

Perry and I speculated as to what they could possibly find. We traveled with all kinds of ideas as to why Sandra would harm Mary, but couldn't come up with any that made sense. We decided to get some lunch in the cafeteria and by the time we were finished, Clark and Paul had joined us.

Clark said he had to get his copter off the roof of the nearby hospital and he and Paul left to find a landing spot for him at the airport. I told Clark that we were returning to Rigby House if they didn't need us any longer, and I knew that Clark would have people checking the Bangor airport for anyone answering her description. We needed to know if she was still in the area because she could be dangerous to us as well.

All was well when we arrived back at Rigby House and we had to alert Rene, Tardy and Gretchen to look out for Sandra. We showed then her picture on Perry's phone.

Chapter 37

My mother had a Boston phone book in the study and I spent the afternoon calling funeral homes to check on any stillborn baby named Charlotte in the timeline that Mary would have given birth. I didn't know whether she had used Ames or Pierce for her last name, but I hit pay dirt on the fifth try. For a shot in the dark, I was lucky. Mary had buried Charlotte Ames Pierce in a local cemetery and the funeral director gave me explicit directions and lot number. I called Granger and asked his help in getting the baby exhumed and prepared for shipment to Tottersham castle to be with her family. I told him that I would like to accompany the baby home to Shea. He said he would take care of it and he called me back two hours later to say it would be arranged for early next week. I felt I had accomplished something today after all. I told Perry I had found Charlotte and he was pleased as well.

Clark called around seven o'clock to say he would be spending the night in Bangor with Paul and they were finding several clues about Sandra. He said an enterprising young officer had tried a seedy car dealership on a hunch and they now knew what kind of car she had been driving. He said they hoped she was still using the same car. They had an all-points bulletin out for the car and Sandra all over the state. She had been staying at a local hotel close to the state hospital and had visited Mary many times over the past week. He felt she was trying to get information as to where Colin was buried and when she had it she killed Mary in retribution for Colin's death.

Clark added that she would probably be heading for Boston and he would keep us informed.

I quickly told him what I had found out about Charlotte and that his father was handling getting the baby's birth certificate and body to take to Shea.

Clark said that we could probably escort Colin and Charlotte together if our luck held with the DNA on the person in the pauper's grave. We would soon know. That was an advantage we had over Sandra in finding Colin.

I told him I loved him and he returned the sentiment and signed off.

I called Frank Vermillion and asked if I could charter his jet sometime next week if all went well with the tests and exhumations. He said no, I couldn't, but he would send his pilots to do whatever and go wherever I wanted to go.

"We are family, Thea, and don't you forget it," he said.

Emmy called and I filled her in on all the happenings and she was totally shocked. We talked for a few minutes and then I went to bed exhausted.

The next day was Saturday and I slept in for a few hours. When the phone rang at nine o'clock I knew it was Clark. He was in Boston and sure enough that was where Sandra had headed. She had been picked up by Boston police when she inquired at the coroner's office about unidentified men and where they would be buried. The coroner's people were right on the ball and called the police. They already had the all-points bulletin from Maine and picked her up and held her for Clark. He was trying to question her now, but she had asked for a lawyer.

"I would love to get some answers from her," Clark said.

"Me too," I said. "She must know plenty."

"While I am right here, I am going to see how the tests are going on the body that we think is Colin. I will also go to the funeral home and get your Baby Charlotte's info that Dad has arranged and everything should go smoothly. We'll fly out of Boston with Colin and Charlotte and that will simplify things. I will arrange for the funeral director who handled Charlotte originally to put her remains in a decent coffin if she isn't already in one and I will also arrange for him to put Colin in a royal casket also for the trip."

I was in tears with gratitude that I had found such a fine human being for my husband and he said he would call later.

144

When Clark arrived at the funeral home he found that the baby's body was already there and they were awaiting instructions. He arranged for a beautiful small cream-colored casket and told the director he hoped to have another for him to prepare for a trip to Europe. The funeral director said he was working with Judge Sanderson in Maine for the proper permits for the transfers and they would be ready when we were. He left the funeral home and went to see Sandra again. She had her lawyer with her and he told them he was preparing to take Colin back to England as soon as the identity was assured.

Sandra gave a great shudder and said, "If you will allow me to accompany Colin's body and my granddaughter's body back to Shea, I will tell you everything I know about Mary's death."

"Sandra, I don't think the Bangor police will allow you to leave the country. You are wanted for murder with them, you know."

She looked at her lawyer and cried, "I have to talk to him, I didn't murder Mary; she was the only family I had left."

Clark also looked at her lawyer and asked, "Do you advise her to talk to me?"

"Mrs. Pierce is under a lot of stress due to finding out her son has been dead all these years. She hasn't killed anyone. She has just been a little foolish," her lawyer said.

"Okay Sandra, I am going to tape this session and anything you say can be held against you in a court of law," Clark said.

"I understand," Sandra said. "My lawyer has advised me of all of that. Let me tell you what happened. When Clara told me that you folks all believed Colin was dead and had been for years I was devastated, but not too surprised. I knew he would have contacted me if he was alive. Clara said that Mary had killed Colin accidentally in a fight and I determined I was going to come find her and have her tell me where his body was so I could bring him home. I left the castle and traveled to Maine and found Mary in the hospital where Clara said they had taken her. I didn't want anyone else to know who I was so I assumed another identity and even bought a car that I could just leave at the airport when I took Colin back. Mary was glad to see me and we talked for hours about Colin. She told me about my granddaughter and where to find her, but she wouldn't tell me where I could find Colin. I cultivated her for days and slowly she began to tell me in pieces about the fight and what had happened to Colin. Her conscience was bothering her a great deal. I had gotten some pills from my doctor to help me sleep and I told Mary about them. I said she ought to ask her doctor for some as well because they were great. On that last day she told me where they had put Colin and I told her she could rest easy because I was going to find him and take him home. I went to the restroom down the hall and left my purse in her room while I was gone. She must have taken my pills because they are gone, but I didn't give them to her. The last time I saw her she was smiling and said she was glad she had told me about Colin and Charlotte. She said I can die happy now. I left her and immediately started for Boston. I didn't know she had taken all the pills and I didn't know she was dead either. I just wanted to find Colin. When the Boston police picked me up I didn't know why they had stopped me, but when I found out she was dead and they were accusing me of killing her, I found out my pills were missing and I was afraid they would accuse me of feeding them to Mary and of course here I am. You have to believe me."

Clark called Paul Decker and talked with him at length about Sandra's story. Paul said they had just got the autopsy report back and she had died of an overdose of sleeping pills. They had found the pill bottle with Sandra's name on it in the trash that had been removed from her room. It had Mary's fingerprints all over it and they were on top of others that had handled the bottle. He assumed they were Sandra's and the pharmacy people. He felt that Sandra's story was consistent with the evidence and as far as he was concerned she was free to go back to England.

The Boston police let Sandra go and she said she would wait to hear from Clark on Monday and gave him her cell phone number and checked into a nearby hotel under her own name. Clark's cell rang and it was the coroner's office. They had just made a positive identification. It was Colin Pierce. He made arrangements for the funeral home to pick him up and told the funeral director they would pick up both bodies on Monday of the following week. He told Sandra they would be leaving on Monday with the caskets and she could go with them on the jet. He then took a cab to the airport, picked up his helicopter and headed for Trafton, Maine.

Chapter 39

When Clark got home on Saturday evening, he had a lot to tell me. He filled me in on all that had happened since he last talked to me and then he called Sheriff Jordan to arrange for time off to again head for England. He talked with Uncle Frank and arranged to leave early Monday morning for Bangor airport and the jet would be ready with two fresh pilots and supplies.

Clark, Perry, and I arrived at Bangor airport with time to spare and we boarded quickly. In no time at all we were in Boston and picking up Sandra who had arrived, per Clark's phone call, by cab, and the two stately coffins of Colin and little Charlotte that arrived by hearses from the funeral home. Sandra sat by herself and spoke very little to any of us. Clark and I were the only ones that conversed during the entire trip. It was a luxury trip all the way, but I arrived at Heathrow tired and weary. I left Clark and Perry to arrange to get the coffins into the waiting hearses and I skipped into a nearby restroom. A pretty little attendant was holding some warm towels when I came out of a stall. She took one look at me and said, "Let me get you some water. In your condition you need to rest." I froze. "In my condition?" I thought.

"What do you mean?" I asked.

"Well, I know that look for sure. My sister-in-law has had five kids and I had to tend to her for all of them. You will do well to rest. You look too stressed."

I wondered why this little attendant would be so concerned about a weary American dressed in jeans and looking very worn and weary.

"You are very kind, but I don't think I am pregnant," I said. "What is your name?"

"I am Abby Willows and I can assure you that you are going to have a baby. Can I help you with anything?" she asked.

I was touched by this young woman's concern for a fellow human with nothing in it for her. She was dressed cleanly but her clothes were much washed and mended. I asked her where she came from and she told me a little place located a few miles out of London. She said her parents had both been killed when she was sixteen and her older brother had taken over the family home and she had been a built-in maid for her sister-in-law. When she was twenty-eight she had asked her brother for a share of the estate so she could get an education and her brother had said she didn't need one as she was fine right where she was. So she had left and had fended for herself here in London for four years. She said she didn't have any skills but was trying to save for a better position in life.

"Where do you live?" I asked.

"I live in a boarding house around the corner. It is not much, but it keeps a roof over my head. I keep looking for new employment but with my background it is difficult. Where do you work?" she asked. She assumed the way I was dressed so casually that I probably also had problems with money.

"I am a librarian in America, but I am headed for my home in Shea, here in England right now. Would you like to be my assistant? If I am indeed going to have a baby, I will need help in all areas of my life and I will pay you well. Let me introduce myself: I am The Marchioness Timothea Claire Chadworth Tottersham Sanderson, but everyone calls me Thea. Will you come to work for me, Abby? How much time do you need to give notice?" I asked.

"I don't need to give notice as there are twenty girls waiting to fill this job but I am leery of giving up this position. I don't know you after all."

"Oh my goodness! Of course you don't. Here let me show you my passport and credentials."

I showed her my identity and she apologized for her suspicion.

"I could really use your help, Abby, and I would like you to come with me now if you can. I am leaving for Shea right now."

Abby's face turned red and she said, "I have to wait until the end of the week so I can pay my rent. I am a little behind. My landlady won't let me have my clothes if I don't pay what I owe her."

"Let's go see her right now and I will pay what you owe. You can take what you want, but we can stop and get anything you need in Shea."

We hurried around the corner and I paid a washed-out looking landlady what Abby owed and she allowed Abby to take her small satchel. We arrived back at the airport to find Clark and Perry pacing back and forth beside the Bentley with worried looks on their faces.

"I am so sorry darling for taking so long, but I have been hiring an assistant and now we are ready to leave," I said.

Clark and Perry stood with their mouths open and I introduced Abby to them. They recovered quickly and shook her hand. Clark raised his brows at me as if to say "What gives?" I gave him my "I'll explain later" look and he just shook his head and smiled.

There was plenty of room in the Bentley for the five of us and we were soon tooling along our way to the castle. Perry had called Clara and she was expecting us. When we arrived as before, the entire workforce was on the steps of the castle to welcome us home. Sandra hurried in and went to her quarters to change for the interment. I introduced an obviously overwhelmed Abby to the staff as my assistant and Clara said she would set up quarters next to my suite for her. I greeted all of the employees on the step and then we went in to change ourselves for the small ceremony. Abby was shown to her quarters, a suite of rooms next to the master suite, for my convenience. I took Clara aside and asked her if she would be able to take Abby to Shea and pick out a wardrobe befitting a woman of her position as my assistant. I told her to spare no expense as Abby would need clothes that would fit all occasions. She would also need personal items and makeup as well as luggage to travel with me. Clara said she would take care of it herself and would have a ball in the bargain. She also knew how to explain it to Abby that the clothes were needed to be able to function as my assistant in all areas of travel so Abby would not feel beholden or embarrassed. Clara was a wise and good woman.

Chapter 40

After changing into suitable clothes for the occasion the castle employees that wanted to, attended the brief interment ceremony for Colin and Charlotte as they were laid to rest beside their relatives in the crypt.

I thought it was time to tell Clark why I had hired an assistant and that he was going to be a papa. We had gone to our suite to rest while Perry took his mother and Abby to Shea to shop.

We went into each other's arms for some much needed attention and then we just relaxed and talked. I put his hand on my naked stomach and said, "You are going to be a father, Clark, what do you think of that?"

He jumped up and shouted, "What?"

I laughed at the look on his face and he grabbed me in his arms and kissed me.

"Are you sure?" he asked.

"Well, Abby assures me that I am and after I thought about it I think she is right." I said.

"I can't wait," Clark said. "Wait until Mother and Dad hear the news. They will be over the moon."

"Are you happy about it?" I asked.

"Are you kidding me? Do you even need to ask? Our own little son or daughter, I am blown away!" he enthused.

We were out in the front court when Perry's vehicle drove into the castle forecourt. The wagon was stacked high and a giggling Clara and Abby tumbled out as a long-suffering Perry looked on.

"Oh, Thea, are you sure you wanted us to spend so much money on me? I am afraid that we went way overboard. I will never be able to wear so many clothes in a million years," said Abby.

"Now, Abby, I told you that there is not one single item that you won't need sooner or later," said Clara. "You will need other articles of clothing that we could not get in Shea, but these will have to do for now. I trust everything will be in order, Thea."

"Clara, I know that you did your best for Abby and we will have to muddle through for now. The rest can wait," I said.

Perry began carrying stacks of boxes and bags to Abby's suite with the help of two footmen. Abby just stood by with tears in her eyes. "Mr. Sanderson, are you sure you wanted your wife to spend so much money on me?" she asked in a timid voice.

Clark just laughed. "I assure you, Abby, Thea does exactly as she pleases and that pleases me. Don't give it another thought. I am a kept man. All the money is hers." He turned and walked off with a smile until he was out of their hearing. Perry who had overheard laughed as well.

Abby looked a little confused, but took it to mean that Clark was okay with the purchases. That made it easier for her to wear the clothes in comfort.

"I will pay you back, Thea. It may take me a few hundred years."

"The wardrobe is a perk of the job, Abby. You will need all of it and more. I don't want to hear another word about it. I think it is time we talked about your duties and wages." I named a wage that left Abby stunned. "You will answer only to me and Clark, but you may take suggestions from others if it will benefit the running of our lives. I intend to see a doctor as soon as we get back to the states and I will depend on your expertise in that department to see that I deliver a strong and healthy heir to Tottersham and the Sanderson dynasty as well. You see, Clark has a fortune of his own. That is why the guys gave you such a leg pull just now. I will need you to help with everything from layette to college. You will earn every penny you are paid and then some. You will be given a suite in Rigby House as well as every other place we visit. You will be given liberal time off and help with any problems you may incur and you will be able to attend any university of your choice. Now, let me see about expediting a visa and passport for you. Perry will take you for pictures when they are ready. Why don't you go help Lucy with getting your wardrobe ready for you to wear? She will be your maid and help you with your clothes when you are here at the castle. I am afraid you will be on your own at Rigby House. We don't have maids there." I laughed.

I called the estate solicitor and asked that he get a passport and visa as soon as possible for Abby. Clara was standing by with all of Abby's particulars and I was surprised to hear her say that Abby's full name was Abigail Helen Willows. She sure had got a lot of info out of Abby; including her date of birth and where she was born, etc. I could see where Perry got his efficiency. Clara had anticipated Abby's need for a passport and had gathered all the information necessary. He told Clara it would be ready for her pictures tomorrow and they made arrangements for Perry to take her. He did not seem to mind all the attention he had to pay to Abby.

Clark had gone to see Herschel and ask if there had been any further problems and Herschel had assured him all was well. Clark knew he could not let his guard down now—too much depended on it. Thea and her precious package were too important to him to allow anything to happen to them.

Chapter 41

We dined in royal splendor that evening and Abby joined us at the table. Her eyes got huge when Perry came in. He was dressed in all his glory in his butler tuxedo and bowed around the table seating us. The twinkle in his eye told me my uncle was thoroughly enjoying his role tonight. I took pity on Abby and explained about Perry's idiosyncrasy. Perry went out roaring with laughter when I said, "That will be all, Granville," thus spoiling his perfect butler façade. He returned after dinner and pulled up a chair next to Abby and acted like it was the normal thing to do. He had coffee with us and we began to talk.

"Uncle Perry, you might be surprised to know that you are going to be a great-uncle. I don't mean as being a good uncle— you are certainly that. I mean as in I am going to have a little heir to the castle. What do you think of that?"

Perry's face went through several changes—from joy to fear to resignation. "Thea, I am so happy for you and Clark as well as for myself, but I have a great fear. Are you sure you want to talk about it around here? We must be prepared for attacks on you and the baby."

"Well, Clark and I have discussed it and we feel that we will not be held hostage as my mother was by not being able to acknowledge our own child. We are going to meet this head on and enjoy our happiness. We hope you will continue to help with protecting the heir."

"You have my word that I will make that my top priority, Thea, as always. Don't you think you owe Abby an explanation?" he asked.

"Yes, I do." I said. "Abby I told you, that you would earn your money and then some so here is the explanation to why that is. A killer has tried to eliminate the heirs to the Tottersham title, and we have to be alert at all times for danger. Anything out of the ordinary cannot be ignored. You will need to be as vigilant as you have ever been for signs of danger. Perry will fill you in and give you many tips. He has been my rock all my life and he will help you understand what is going on here at the castle. When we return to America, we hope the danger there has been erased, but we can't be sure. My mother and father were both murdered and if you want to return to London, I will find you employment that will allow you to further your education. It could be very dangerous for you with me."

Abby sat as though she was stunned. "I am so sorry that someone has done this to you, Thea. I would never think to leave you if you need my help. I will listen to what Perry has to say and we will both try to protect you. I know already that you are a good person and there are not enough of you in the world."

"Hear, hear!" Perry raised his cup and we all toasted Abby. She blushed and we turned to the topic of what we would be doing for the next couple of days.

Clark and Perry went about the business of the estate and checked everything from the books to the gates on the paddocks. Perry wanted Clark to know what was expected of him as a fellow steward of the Tottersham realm. Clark was a quick study and asked questions that surprised Perry. Herschel had gone off to do something else and they were in the estate office. Clark had asked about overhead costs and how they could easily be taken advantage of in the wrong hands. He asked if there shouldn't be a common checks and balances on the entire estate, including the holdings in Africa and elsewhere, just to be efficient—not that he didn't trust Herschel. If Perry said he was golden than that was good enough for Clark. Perry said he would think about it and went off with a thoughtful look on his face.

I spent the day adjusting to being lady of the castle again and showing Abby the royal ropes so to speak. She was very intelligent and wanted to learn everything at once. She was self-educated and very well read. She knew poetry and all about current events and politics. She had studied books about the royal families and knew quite a bit about royal protocol. Thea wasn't surprised—she had known that Abby was a gem and was so glad she had met her. She was going to be a great help to her.

Clark and Perry were just coming out of the estate office when Herschel came in the side door. Abby and I were standing in the hall having just come down from inspecting a possible nursery site upstairs near our suites. It was comical that we all converged at the same time. Herschel was looking at Perry and Clark and Abby was looking at Herschel. I watched all of them with little interest, but later Abby asked Perry who Herschel was and why he was looking at Clark and Perry with such apprehension. I overheard her asking Perry the question and asked one of my own.

"Did you find anything wrong with the books, Perry?"

"No, Clark and I just took a more in-depth look than I usually do and he pointed out some things that I might need to correct with the estate business both here and abroad. I never gave it much thought, but Herschel is not getting any younger and we might need to have a more efficient way to do things in case someone else has to take over. I will talk to him about it."

"I just thought he looked like someone with his hand in the cookie jar," said Abby.

"From the mouths of the innocent," mused Clark with a thoughtful look.

Perry just looked disturbed and went into the office and closed the door.

I noticed that Clark was being awfully pensive for him and I wondered if he and Perry had stirred up a hornet's nest without realizing it.

I began to notice that Herschel was a regular fixture, coming and going by the side door so much that nobody even took notice of him. Could it be possible that my father had noticed some discrepancies with the accounts? Where was Herschel when my father died? I talked with Clark about it and he said he had been thinking the same thing and unless he was greatly mistaken so was Perry.

The next day I did notice that Perry spent an inordinate amount of time in the office making calls to the branch estates. He said he was talking to the managers about checks and balances and they did not have a system in place. He began to promptly install a new system with Clark over the internet with the different branches. Clark was very interested in what a manager in Africa had to say. He said that Lord Randall had asked the same questions just before he had had his accident with a load of grain spilling from a silo and burying him. It was a while before anyone found him. He said Mr. Herschel was so upset he closed the plant for a week. Perry looked at Clark and they both knew what the other was thinking. Herschel had been in Africa with Randall when he was killed. "Had the killings been about finance and not inheritance?"

They quickly installed the same system on the castle books and waited for Herschel to comment. It didn't take long for him to erupt when he checked the books at the end of the day.

"What the hell is going on? I have to log in and out and enter every change I make to the day's exchanges? Do you trust me or not, Perry?" he yelled.

"It is not a matter of trust, Herschel. We have to look to the future and anticipate change. I think it is a good idea and we will get used to it in no time. It is what Clark wants and we will go with it."

"I am not so stupid that I don't know when I am being questioned about my honesty. I have dealt with this before."

"You mean when Lord Randall questioned you about the books in Africa?" Clark asked.

"I don't know what you are talking about. Randall trusted me completely," he barked.

"I don't think so. He did question you and a few hours later he was mysteriously dead. A grain silo collapsed that had been reliable for years and the men had been sent to the other side of the estate that day. You were there though weren't you, Herschel? You watched him die in a pile of grain because he caught you cooking the books. Did Lord Tim catch you too, Herschel? Is that why he had to go over the parapet tower? Was he making provisions for his new wife and found the discrepancies, too? It makes sense that you would be with him while he inspected the castle walls and roofs. You didn't need any stealth, did you? Tim would have turned his back on you just like Randall. Was it worth it, Herschel, to kill two good men who had given you the run of their estate? Have you slept soundly in your bed these past thirty years? You unleashed a firestorm that ruined the childhood of a beautiful little girl. You allowed poor Colin Pierce to take the suspicion of killing his brother and ruining his life as well as his mother's and wife. Because you let him take the fall, Thea's mother was murdered as well by Colin's deranged wife. Are you happy, Hershel? Was it worth it? If you needed the money any one of them would have given it to you—you didn't need to steal it from them. You surely didn't need to murder them."

I watched from the doorway with Abby by my side as Herschel shriveled before Clark's onslaught.

"I don't have to answer to you. You have no jurisdiction here, Lieutenant," he sneered.

"No, Mr. Dennis, but I do." The words came from Inspector Hood who had been waiting behind me listening to the exchange. "You are under arrest for suspicion of murder in the first degree on two counts. I don't think we will have much trouble convicting you, sir. Now come along peaceably.

Herschel was removed from the castle that he had betrayed. We were all stunned that it was over—all because my little assistant Abby had caught a look and was not afraid to voice her opinion. Clark and Perry would have gotten there eventually but Abby certainly speeded things up.

We all stayed at the castle with Perry while he worked with the new manager. It proved to be enlightening for us all. Perry continued to not mind Abby. Clara was thrilled. Clark and I thought about our baby every day. I went to see a doctor in London and was told that there would be a conflict of heirs in the future because it all depended on which of our babies was born first—there would be three boys growing up in the castle again! Sylvia and Granger came to stay to be sure their triplet grandbabies were well taken care of. They didn't need to worry as Abby was on duty.

Back in Trafton, Sheriff Jordan had extended Clark's leave of absence. Andrew and Temple continued to fight. Uncle Hal had scared Carry onto the straight and narrow and Emmy was happy with her new role as head librarian. She and Bruce were thinking of planning a wedding. Rene was cooking up a storm for Tardy and Gretchen. Arabella and Frank buzzed back and forth from Britain to Washington D.C. and there was talk of the presidency. Hillary had left for parts unknown—and nobody seemed to care.

About the Author

Marti Brann, writing as Delia Drake, was born and raised in Maine and thinks it is the nicest place on earth. She has many interests including raising show chickens with her long-suffering husband. She is an avid reader and likes to work out of doors. She prefers mowing the lawn and helping with the vegetable garden to doing housework, but her husband picks up the slack. Delia's stories come from a vivid imagination that has entertained her family for years. She decided to share with others and hopes they enjoy reading them as much as she enjoys writing them. She lives in Vassalboro, Maine, with her husband Austin; the spirit of a very spoiled long-haired Chihuahua named Adrian; a very plump black cat named Rachel Rose; and her newest baby, a Pomeranian named Paisley. Delia can be reached at DeliaDrake@roadrunner.com.

CPSIA information can be obtained
at www.ICGtesting.com
Printed in the USA
BVOW06s1840020117
472375BV00001B/46/P